"Stop Playing the Untouched Virgin!"

Caleb sneered. "My brother told his wife your weekend together wasn't planned. She didn't believe those lies—and neither do I."

"You weren't even there," Diana snapped, anger replacing her fear. "I've heard you're cold-blooded, ruthless . . . well, at least your brother was warm—"

It was a challenge that had to be met. His face changed from anger and indifference to a look of unmasked desire—for her.

He stepped closer, his eyes seeming to strip the clothes from her body. "Maybe I wouldn't mind taking up where my brother left off. . . ."

DANA TERRILL
has written her first Silhouette Romance, *Man of Velvet*, which won the 1981 Golden Heart Award in the Romantic Writers of America contest. Dana, who is as lively as her heroines, lives and writes in Salt Lake City.

Dear Reader:

I'd like to take this opportunity to thank you for all your support and encouragement of Silhouette Romances.

Many of you write in regularly, telling us what you like best about Silhouette, which authors are your favorites. This is a tremendous help to us as we strive to publish the best contemporary romances possible.

All the romances from Silhouette Books are for you, so enjoy this book and the many stories to come. I hope you'll continue to share your thoughts with us, and invite you to write to us at the address below:

Karen Solem
Editor-in-Chief
Silhouette Books
P.O. Box 769
New York, N.Y. 10019

DANA TERRILL
Man of Velvet

Silhouette *Romance*

Published by Silhouette Books New York

America's Publisher of Contemporary Romance

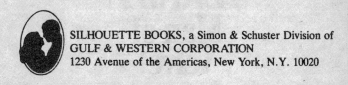 SILHOUETTE BOOKS, a Simon & Schuster Division of
GULF & WESTERN CORPORATION
1230 Avenue of the Americas, New York, N.Y. 10020

ISBN: 0-671-57181-8

First Silhouette Books printing October, 1982

10 9 8 7 6 5 4 3 2 1

Map by Ray Lundgren

Man of
Velvet

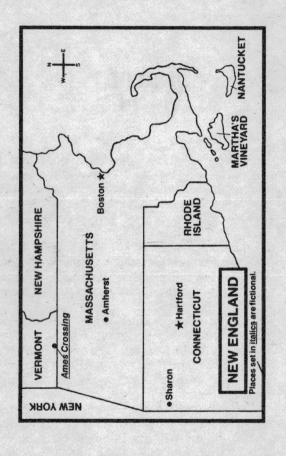

NEW YORK

VERMONT NEW HAMPSHIRE

Ames Crossing

MASSACHUSETTS

• Amherst Boston ★

CONNECTICUT

• Sharon Hartford ★

RHODE ISLAND

MARTHA'S VINEYARD

NANTUCKET

N
W E
S

NEW ENGLAND
Places set in italics are fictional.

Chapter One

Diana Lacklain stepped from the close confinement of her car. She'd been sitting there for some time trying to gather the courage to commit an act of burglary. While not exactly breaking and entering—she did have a key—if caught she'd have a difficult time explaining what she was doing there.

Gusty April winds whipped the long strands of her hair loose from her scarf and made it almost impossible for her to see. She brushed them back with an impatient hand before tightening the belt of her raincoat, fortifying herself to do what she must.

The moon appeared occasionally through the dark, ominous clouds. Soon they would draw a curtain completely across its brightness. Diana was careful to avoid falling as she picked her way cautiously along the unkempt path. It would be a disaster to break a leg out here miles from home.

When she finally reached the concealment of a group of trees that served as a windbreak, she paused to take a closer look at the two-story Tudor-style house. The dark brown crisscrossed wainscoting was stark against the white stuccoed walls. A weekend country estate, it was unoccupied, she understood, except for an older couple who lived on the premises year round. It was after midnight and they should be asleep upstairs, well away from the library. Just a few steps ahead were the french doors. The key to the door lay in the palm of her hand—cold, sharp metal that cut into her flesh as she gripped it tightly.

Diana felt unfamiliarly light-headed, and was sure she would soon give way to an insane desire to laugh. Her absurd sense of humor cropped up at the most unlikely times.

Honestly, Diana, you would make a rotten thief, she thought. *You jump like a skittish colt at every branch that moves.*

The biting wind was chilling her to the bone, and knowing it was now or never, she forced herself to take the few remaining steps to the door. Carefully she fitted the key in the lock and turned it slowly. She felt a certain satisfaction when it sprang open with a low click. Trembling, she turned the knob and stepped soundlessly inside, convinced after a few moments that the room was unoccupied. The only easily discernible sign of previous use was the glow of coals from the banked fire.

Diana paused still another moment, hearing only the ticking of a grandfather clock, the pendulum making a swishing sound as it moved back and forth—that plus an occasional hiss from the fire. Slowly her eyes became accustomed to the dark room and she was able to make out the various shapes of furniture—the sofa, two wing chairs, and finally, *the* desk.

It was a massive piece in mahogany finish, with a writing pad, globe, desk lamp and phone sitting on top. She felt deeper into her pocket for the smaller key, which would open the desk drawer.

Cautiously Diana took her first steps across the room, her shoes making a faint clicking sound on the hardwood floor. Her footsteps were accompanied by a

8

loud clap of thunder and the first drops of rain, which pinged against the french doors she had just closed.

Quietly Diana knelt by the desk, waiting, listening, before fitting the key in the drawer. She gave it a sharp twist before she tugged at the drawer, which, momentarily, stuck when she tried to open it. At last, it opened, but not without making a scraping noise.

She paused again . . . listening.

Hearing nothing, she clicked on a small penlight and saw at once that the bundle of letters she had come to recover were obstructing the drawer. Diana immediately recognized the handwriting on the envelopes. They were supposed to be in the back of the drawer, hidden from view, but she didn't pause to speculate about what they were doing here in plain sight.

Snapping off the flashlight, she shut the drawer and prepared to relock it when she was suddenly spun around by two powerful hands on her shoulders. She was sent sprawling across the top of the desk, pushing most of the objects on it to the floor with a loud crash.

Dismayed, she gasped, her breath driven from her as a powerful male body landed squarely on top of her. Diana was so overwhelmed with the suddenness of the attack that she experienced a loud buzzing noise inside her head. Silently she struggled with a mind-boggling fear that threatened to make her lose consciousness.

The light-headedness passed after a moment. Diana felt a hard, lean jawline against her face as the owner of it reached across her to click on the desk lamp.

From the angle that Diana first laid eyes on Caleb Buchanan, the shadows gave him a diabolical appearance. With only inches separating them, the light cast the sharp planes of his face into harsh, austere lines. The hardness was inherent in the grim angle of his mouth, the dark fury alive in his eyes. She knew immediately who he was!

9

With a penetrating thoroughness his gaze swept over his captive, widening with disbelief as he murmured, "Well, a lady cat burglar!"

His hand reached up and pulled the scarf from her head, and her long honey-colored hair cascaded over his arm with the motion. His sharp, chestnut-brown eyes traveled slowly over her features, taking note of each one and drinking in their loveliness. Dark, hazel-green eyes, alive with fear, appeared more green than gray. His gaze continued to the high, delicate cheekbones, the slim patrician nose, and lingered on the warm trembling lips.

He raised his body from hers and Diana saw the lean, powerful body that had held her captive. Well-developed chest muscles outlined his hard torso covered by a thick mat of curly russet-brown hair. He was a prime specimen of manhood. The only flaw to his physique was a wicked scar that stretched across his flat stomach and disappeared into the ridiculously short towel that encircled his waist.

She heard him say, "Well now, let's find out what you hoped to find. Most of the valuable pieces aren't here—this is just a weekend retreat. Sorry to disappoint you." He smiled wickedly. "There are some heirloom furnishings, 'collector's' items, . . . but nothing you could possibly plan to carry off. So what were you after? Especially in the desk? There's nothing of value there but . . . wait a minute. . . ." He paused, an idea coming to mind. Bending down he pulled open the drawer, which was supposed to be locked.

He had locked it himself—and it didn't look forced.

Their eyes clashed. Every formidable detail Diana had ever heard about Caleb Buchanan was embodied in his being. Never had she seen such anger; he exuded it, as the realization of who she was and what she was after dawned on him.

Diana knew what she would see if she looked in the mirror—her face would be white. Her fear intensified.

"The letters? Where are they?" His voice chilled her with its coldness.

"On the floor," she said with husky breathlessness, as she spoke for the first time and gestured to where they had landed moments before. She judged the distance between them and the time it would take her to have the letters in her possession and be out the door.

"I wouldn't try it if I were you! You wouldn't even make it halfway," he warned, guessing accurately at what she was thinking. His voice was a velvet-edged sword. "Hand them over or wish you had."

She knew he would accept nothing but strict compliance, so she did as she was told, at the same time being careful to avoid any contact with him.

"I've already glanced through them anyway," he snapped. "Full of nothing but sentimental tripe."

"They weren't meant for your eyes."

"Only my buffoon of a brother. You really had him wrapped around your little finger, didn't you? He was ready to give up everything to run off with you. I was on my way back to knock some sense into him when word came that it was already too late. He was dead and his wife is in a wheelchair for the rest of her life." This last was stated with such venom that Diana cringed visibly under the onslaught. "Tell me," he went on, "the way you signed them, the letter 'D'; what does it stand for?"

"Diana," she whispered, noting the conclusion he'd drawn and seeing no reason to enlighten him.

He laughed mirthlessly. "That's rich. Diana, Goddess of the Hunt, and Barrett such easy prey! Well, let's see what the rest of you looks like. Take off your coat."

He walked around the desk, allowing Diana to see

11

for the first time the rest of his body, perfect in its symmetry. Endowed with a physique and balance an Olympic athlete would have envied, he looked as if he could run for days and never tire, never even draw a deep breath.

Nervous, she replied hesitantly, "I'd rather leave it on, thanks."

"I said, take it off!" He took a step toward her and she knew he wouldn't be averse to doing it himself. Trembling, she did as he ordered, not daring to speculate as to the reason why.

Alert to his derisive mockery, she endured what she had to as his eyes slid boldly over her contours, taking note of her slenderness and delicate bones, his gaze lingering on the fullness of her breasts and slender hips. She felt naked under his mocking look, just as he wanted her to feel.

"Please, would you go put something on," she asked, her voice barely audible. Instantly she regretted the words, but she was unable to endure the way he was taunting her.

He touched the scant toweling wraparound. "Is this bothering you? You've seen a man in less . . . or are you still going to pretend to be the *un*touched virgin?" He paused to sneer. "My brother could be very naive for an adult male. He tried to convince his wife that your weekend together wasn't planned. But she wasn't taken in by your fabricated lies and neither was I."

"You weren't there! How do you know so much about it?" Diana snapped, angry for the first time, forgetting her fear. "Maybe it was totally innocent, at first. Emotions have been known to get out of hand. I've heard what a cold-blooded, absolutely ruthless person you are. Well, your brother was cut from a different bolt of cloth! He was genuine and warm, more

12

deserving of happiness than most." Truly enraged now, her eyes flashed their deepest green, moist with emotion. She spat at him. "Cold-blooded is too mild, ice water would be more like it!"

It was too much of a taunt, a challenge that could not go unanswered. Suddenly, his expression changed from cold remote anger and indifference to one she'd seen too many times to have it go unrecognized. His eyes blazed with unmasked desire.

He stepped closer. "You needn't act with me. I know too much about you." His eyes stripped the clothes from her body as he said softly, almost to himself, "Maybe I wouldn't mind taking up where my brother left off!"

His hands closed over her wrists, dragging her against the solid wall of his chest. The weight of his arms held her in a vise before his searing mouth took possession of hers, his hand coming up to cup the fullness of her breast underneath her sweater.

With sickening swiftness she knew without a doubt that he had no intention of stopping. What better way of showing his low opinion of her morals? Her thoughts racing ahead, and fighting sheer terror, Diana knew that he would probably enjoy her meager efforts, that he would like nothing better than to have her fight him.

It took every ounce of will power she possessed to remain impassive. Deliberately she kept her body stiff, showing no response despite his experienced touch. Deep inside she could feel a flicker of awareness and she had to fight that too. He definitely knew what he was doing.

Endlessly, his kiss continued. The storm raging outside, a silent battle of wills going on within. Diana knew she had to make him stop. Any more of this and she'd scream.

As mockingly as possible, she tilted her head to one side, her voice dripping with sarcasm. "I'm afraid, Caleb, you haven't your brother's technique."

The change in him was instantaneous. He dropped his arms, his eyes once again full of cold contempt. He said with barely repressed anger, "You'd better get out of here while you still can." He threw the letters and her coat at her. "And you'd be advised to *stay* away from me in the future."

She fled into the night.

Before she had gone a dozen steps she was soaked, the wind wildly whipping her hair about, driving the rain at her face. Twice she stumbled, sinking into the oozing mud. An eternity later she found her car.

Never one to give way to tears, it took all her strength to keep from surrendering to the hysteria inside. She drove away, her lips pressed tightly together, eyes burning with unshed tears. She hardly remembered the long drive home—only the blackness of the night.

Even now, more than two years later, a stormy night still unsettled her. The present storm made her restless. Unable to concentrate, Diana finally gave up and laid the book she'd been trying to read aside. Standing up, she walked to the window and gazed out at the approaching storm. It was absurd to try to follow the drift of the story. She'd read the same passage three times and not once had it made any sense.

Thunderstorms always had the same effect—a portentous feeling of apprehension that Diana couldn't shrug away. The first distant roll of thunder caused the unwelcome change, one that continued until the storm abated, making her recall that night no matter how hard she tried not to.

Turning, she walked into the small kitchen. Maybe a

glass of warm milk would relax the tension and act as a tranquilizer, help her to sleep.

Later, having polished off the last of the warm milk, Diana felt certain she'd be able to slip into the arms of Morpheus without any more visitations from the past.

After rinsing the mug and pan, she turned them upside down on the drainboard. Next, she wiped the counter and clicked off the light before going to check on Barry. She found him asleep, oblivious to the thunderstorm, in his usual position—totally uncovered with his little bottom high in the air, his thumb conveniently near his mouth.

He should sleep, she thought fondly! At the ripe old age of one and a half, he never seemed to stop running the whole day, with the exception of a very short nap. It wasn't easy keeping up with an inexhaustible bundle of energy. Not easy, but well worth the effort. She gave the baby a pat before covering him and going to her own room.

Her thoughts turned to her work. With a little luck she'd finish the illustrations within the week. Then she'd travel to Boston where she would sign a contract for her art work. The contract should make the future a lot more secure.

Dropping her dressing gown at the end of the bed, she slipped between the cool sheets and forced her body to relax. The tranquilizing effect of the warm milk took over, lulling her to sleep almost instantly.

But it wasn't a restful night. Her dreams were dominated by a shadow from the past. She seemed to be forever running, as fast as she could, while behind her a man with chestnut-brown eyes effortlessly followed.

Chapter Two

Spring at last was well established with the stormy days of March gone. April flowers were in full flourish and the Vermont countryside was green with promise after the record-breaking snow levels of the previous winter.

There, that should do it, she thought as she packed the last of her illustrations in the portfolio. She stretched, relaxing after the intense concentration. Pleased, Diana smiled, giving herself a mental pat on the back. She had finished exactly on schedule. Tomorrow she would be traveling by train to Boston to deliver the finished product and complete the final negotiations before signing the contract with a publisher—a promise of steady income for her art. This was very different from the frightening first months when she'd found herself on her own with an infant depending solely on her for sustenance.

She'd been lucky.

First of all, she had found a place to live. She and Barry had left Connecticut and had gone as far as her money could take them soon after her encounter with Caleb Buchanan on that stormy April night two years ago. She'd planned to leave anyway—he had simply hastened the departure.

At least she'd managed to put the state of Massachusetts between her and that detestable man. It was doubtful they would ever meet again. Ames Crossing was a small farm community in a sparsely populated area of Vermont, far from New England's large cities. She had begun to feel relatively safe here.

It had turned out to be good fortune when her old car had decided to get temperamental and not run at all just when she was passing through this small town. One thing had led to another after the garage man called a couple who had an old farmhouse they might possibly rent, and within the hour Diana had decided to stay.

Jeffery and Martha Burnside were a godsend. Jeff was a veterinarian with an established practice and boarding kennels. Diana was able to keep his books and help with the feeding of the animals on weekends and holidays in lieu of rent. Jeff and Marty shared with them the vegetables from a large garden, as well as their natural friendliness.

Parents of two small boys of their own, Ricky and Joey, ages five and six respectively, the Burnsides gave her child-rearing hints and exchanged babysitting with her. Marty was going to watch Barry during Diana's overnight stay in Boston. He was shy with strangers, not having seen many in his small lifetime. On his horizon Ricky and Joey were star attractions. Barry would toddle to them with a big grin as they very patiently entertained him. They wouldn't hesitate to cart out the whole box of toys when he showed even the slightest boredom with any one thing.

The next morning Barry was only half-awake as Diana took him across the farmyard. Soft and cuddly, his brown curls had a decided reddish cast in the morning sun. He snuggled closer in her arms, making it infinitely harder for her to give him over to Marty.

Her eyes full of understanding, Marty told her, "I remember having to leave Joey, too. *Three whole days,* while I was in the hospital having Rick. The doctor wanted me to stay longer . . . but no way. I insisted on coming home, sure that Joey was pining away. He almost ignored me and went right on with what he was doing. Very ego shattering!"

Diana knew Marty's words were meant to make her feel better about leaving Barry, but she would be glad when she was on her way back from Boston.

She half listened as Jeffery drove her to the station and waved good-bye as the train pulled out. He promised to pick her up when she returned and said he would bring Barry as well as the whole family.

All the luggage she had was a garment bag with numerous pockets and the large portfolio with her illustrations and sketches inside. Once these were stowed away in the overhead compartment, she settled back with her ever present sketch pad and a few magazines she'd brought along.

It was a long and uneventful trip, and Diana was glad to see the outskirts of Boston. By the time she'd refreshed her makeup, the train was at the station only a few minutes behind schedule.

She was met at the station by Steve Brenner, one of the young executives of the firm she was to be associated with. He was good-looking, with dark hair and a moustache. His piercing blue eyes sparkled with hidden laughter as he said with disbelief, almost to himself, "And to think I didn't particularly want to come!"

Diana smiled, liking his honesty. "Then why did you?" she asked.

"Mainly because I'm not the boss; merely an 'up and coming' with a long way to go before I get to the top. In this case, I'm glad they insisted," he grinned.

He helped her into his low-slung sports car, a canary-yellow Porsche 928. With an air of savoir faire and a speed that made Diana uncomfortable, Steve maneuvered his way through the heavy traffic.

"In case you noticed, my last name is the same as Brenner Publishing. My father owns it. But don't get any ideas I'm a softie with a cushy job. I started at the bottom—the *very* bottom. My degree is in journalism and I worked part-time to learn the ropes while attending the University of Massachusetts. I know one day it will all be mine, but Dad will make sure I earn it."

"You seem defensive."

"Sorry, I guess I am. There have been more than a few comments lately about 'Baby Blue Eyes finding Daddy's shoes rather large.'"

"Are they too large?"

"Yes," he said laughing, "but they're getting smaller. You'd like to have a tour of the company, wouldn't you?" he asked. At her affirmative nod, he continued, "And I'd like nothing better than to show you around and 'off' to the rest of the wolves who were more than willing to send me as 'errand boy.'" He laughed, already enjoying the anticipated look of disbelief he'd see on their faces. "I bet next time someone needs to be picked up at the train station they'll have a dozen takers."

They both laughed.

He added, "How about an evening on the town? There's a new restaurant on the wharf which I've heard has an excellent chef. Besides, I *vaunt* to be alone with you," he said, with a Dracula-like leer.

"Yes, I'd like that. *I think!*" Diana replied enthusiastically, liking his natural manner, his friendliness. It had been a while since she'd spent an evening in the company of an attractive man. She suspected that Steve Brenner was a charmer.

"Great!" he grinned, pleased that this honey-colored vision didn't have a ring on the third finger of her left hand. "And don't worry about a place to stay, I'll handle it."

The afternoon passed quickly. The publishing company was a fascinating business to observe, especially with a knowledgeable guide. It was easy to see where Steve Brenner got his charm. His father's personality was forceful, but friendly, and his employees were amiable and relaxed in his presence. Diana knew intuitively that she could respect and trust his business acumen.

With the contract signed, Robert Brenner insisted she stay with them. "My wife would love it. Besides, there are just the three of us rambling around in that big old house."

Diana turned to Steve, with an accusing look, thinking he must have instigated the whole thing. He held up his hands in self-defense. "Honest Injun . . . Dad thought of it. I swear!" He grinned easily. "Only I couldn't have thought of a better idea myself."

Diana hesitated only a moment before agreeing to stay, and a short time later they were sweeping up the drive of a stately old home in a suburb of Boston. Impressed by the house, Diana began to feel ill at ease with the grandeur of the place. She mentioned it to Steve.

"Relax. This will be painless." And it proved true.

Charlotte Brenner was a gracious and charming woman with beautiful iron-gray hair and the soft remnant of a Southern drawl. She greeted Diana warmly.

"Welcome, my dear. We love having you, though I personally doubt we'll see much of you, *if* I know my son!"

"You're absolutely right there, Mother," Steve agreed. "We are going out. There isn't much time to prove how witty and full of charm I can be. Of course," he added with his usual ready grin, "she's already half-convinced."

"Your charm and wit are exceeded only by your modesty," Diana smiled.

"She has you pegged," Charlotte smiled, amused by their easy bantering.

Mrs. Brenner showed her to the guest room and left her. Diana hung the weekender bag in the closet. She took the cosmetics out of the side pockets, along with a change of clothing, nightgown, and toiletries. They were the only things she'd brought.

It proved to be a thoroughly enjoyable evening and she had little time to think about missing Barry. A few hours of masculine attention did wonders for any girl's ego, and Diana wasn't different from most. During the last two years, she'd been so involved with child rearing that she'd discouraged any man who came too close. Ames Crossing wasn't exactly brimming over with eligible men. Even so, there she had had a few arranged dates set up by would-be matchmakers—but nothing had resulted but friendship.

As she glanced around the restaurant full of elegantly dressed women, Diana began to feel very concerned about what she considered her inappropriate "little black dress." She whispered, under her breath, "Steve Brenner, I am very underdressed! You shouldn't have brought me here."

Steve reassured her, "You'd look great in anything." Then, eyeing her, he continued with wicked amusement, "or nothing!"

She colored slightly under the gleam in his eye, enjoying his flirting. His flattery was harmless, at least she hoped so.

It seemed a natural culmination to a very enjoyable evening to allow him to turn her easily in his arms and kiss her thoroughly, but pleasantly. Declining a nightcap, she kissed him again, glad he was keeping the end of the evening as delightful as the rest had been. She knew Steve wasn't nearly so much the lightweight he presented himself as. He'd been bruised a bit, too.

"Hey, you're miles away while I'm here pressing my most amorous and ardent suit."

"You've kissed the Blarney Stone, Steven Brenner. More than once I'd fancy," she added, disengaging her arms. "It is late. We should get to bed." When he grinned with obvious delight, she quickly amended, "No, don't you dare make something of that remark. You can see how sleepy and slow-witted I am. I enjoyed myself. Goodnight."

The next day when he took her to the train station, Steve asked if he could call her. At her hesitation, he continued, "You can have lots of elbow room."

"Let me think about it. Okay?" she said lightly.

"Okay," he agreed, his eyes intensely blue, "only promise not to keep me waiting too long."

"I promise."

Hands on her shoulders, he kissed her before she stepped aboard the train. She waved, then disappeared into the coach. From the window of the train, Diana watched Steve walk back to the parking lot, two steps at a time. She could almost hear him whistling.

She liked him. The atmosphere over dinner the night before had been warm and friendly. He had a dry wit that especially appealed to her funny bone. It was the kind of humor Diana loved to indulge in. The subdued atmosphere of the restaurant hadn't encouraged loud laughter, and at times Diana had felt hard pressed to keep from giving in to the bubble inside. Steve could take exception to almost everything.

He'd had a rough time of it once. Although he hadn't gone into great detail, she knew his girl had married someone else. "I had trouble," he'd said, in an unusually serious voice, "dealing with the fact that although she was everything to me, it wasn't reciprocated on her part. She married my best friend."

Lasting relationships hadn't been Diana's experience, either. It still amazed her how easy Steve had been to talk with. She'd told him things she'd never even told her sister.

Shortly after Diana and her sister had moved to Hartford, Diana had gotten the lead in a summer stock play. "I was pretty stupid," she'd said to Steve, "and a *very young* nineteen. The leading man was quite *devastatingly* good-looking, and in my 'tender' heart he quickly became my ideal of a future husband. We were inseparable during the weeks of the rehearsal, and I was sure he must love me as much as I thought I loved him. Then one day I overheard a conversation between him and another member of the cast.

"Essentially, they had a wager going, and it seemed my leading man was under the impression he was about to collect. In the thick of my first love affair, I was devastated. It seems like such trivia now, but at the time, I remember how I used to lie awake nights and plot his slow and painful demise."

With a look of mock horror on his face, Steve said, "I'm certainly glad it wasn't me."

"I'm glad too," Diana said with a laugh, liking his sense of humor. "You're much too nice."

"Look how much you're improving in your judgment of character. And I am going to see it continues. Who knows where your good taste could lead!"

"Who knows," she echoed as they toasted their beginnings.

All in all, it had been a delightful evening. If he did call she decided she would like to see him, although the distance from Boston to Ames Crossing might put a damper on frequent visits.

Diana stored her overnight luggage and the now

empty portfolio in the overhead rack and once again prepared herself for the long trip home. It seemed endless.

In the middle of the afternoon she changed trains. The next two hours seemed endless as she longed to catch her first glimpse of Barry. At last, with only minutes to spare before arriving in Ames Crossing, Diana freshened her appearance, ran a comb through her hair and touched lipstick to her mouth. She stood up, pulled her things from above, and walked the length of the coach car to step into the bright sunlight.

She wasn't to know until later that the unusual color of her hair caught the eye of a man in another train that had just arrived.

Twice a day at Ames Crossing the arrival of a train from upstate New York was scheduled to coincide with that of a train coming from either the east or the south. This railroad was known for its slow, tedious journeys —especially to passengers accustomed to jet-age travel.

For the man in the other train, it had been a wasted journey. The couple had changed their minds about selling the antique chest for which he'd expressly made the trip. It had been a particularly fine example of a "William and Mary" chest of burl hardwood, made in the late 1600s. This family heirloom was a rare find and had received only tender loving care. At the last minute the owners had decided against selling it. And then his car had broken down in some "spot-in-the-road" town with no parts or service!

He wasn't in the best of moods.

Scowling, he looked at the girl, her face hidden from view. The rich, rare color of her hair—honey streaked with gold—reminded him of Diana, the person he believed responsible for his brother's death. It was a memory that didn't do much for his already short temper.

She turned her head, as if she were looking for someone, and for the first time, he saw her face and he stared at her.

It was Diana!

His dark eyes narrowed as he watched. He still couldn't believe it! She'd lost none of her beauty in the two years since they'd met. If anything, she was even more beautiful in the bright light of day.

Suddenly she dropped the bundles in her arms. Dismayed, the man watched a slow transformation on her face. She smiled, genuine delight in her expression, arms open to embrace someone.

His eyes shifted to see who it was.

What Caleb Buchanan saw was a group of people—a family—a man, woman, and three small children—all smiling in Diana's direction. The woman carried a small boy, the youngest of the three. She put him down— actually she didn't have much choice the way he was wiggling and squirming in her arms.

Suddenly the man in the train sat up, his brown eyes mesmerized by what he saw.

The small child toddled as fast as his short legs could carry him toward Diana, who waited, arms out- stretched. She squatted down to an available height for the two chubby arms that now encircled her neck. Then she stood up, whirling around in obvious enjoyment. The bright russet-colored curls of the child were only a couple of feet from the train window, his head on Diana's shoulder, held tightly there by her hand at the back of his neck.

Caleb Buchanan stared in disbelief, watching as Diana held the child away from her, laughing up at his toothy grin. Once again, she hugged him close. The reddish-brown eyes of the child and the russet color of his hair were identical to his own. Anyone seeing the child and himself together would have thought the boy was his instead of his brother's.

Caleb continued to watch them as they exchanged greetings, the older man in the family helping Diana with her things since she had her hands full with the child. As the man turned, Caleb saw the imprint "Burnside Veterinary" on the back of his coveralls—something he'd need to know if he expected to locate her.

Ames Crossing, he mused, a small New England town where everyone knew everyone else. He knew where to find her now, and when he did he wanted an element of surprise. He didn't want any possibility of her disappearing into thin air.

It wouldn't take more than a few minutes on the phone to find out where she lived. He had the connections, and when he found her he would be the one calling the shots!

Any one single incident in his travel plans could have changed the entire encounter. He'd decided on the train after his car had broken down and he'd missed the only regular scheduled airline in a two-hundred-mile radius. How he'd hated the slowness of the train, the noisy teenagers in the same car. He'd fumed mile after mile over his bad luck. Now this! Caleb settled back in his seat, trying to digest the few things he knew to be fact.

First of all, the child must be around a year and a half. Diana must have been about four months pregnant when he'd seen her last and the child must have been conceived during the weekend she and Barrett had spent together at Woodledge.

He should have read all those letters!

The fact of her pregnancy was probably why she'd pressed Barrett for a divorce, desperate at the prospect of having the child alone. Or, Caleb thought cynically, at least some monetary compensation would have been nice. There was still the missing money—a large cash withdrawal—which had never been accounted for, and which had been taken from Barrett's savings account two weeks before he died.

There had always been a few elements missing, and now he knew where to find the answers.

Chapter Three

The first thing Diana was to recall about the morning was that it began uneventfully.

She had managed an almost uninterrupted hour at her easel, since Marty had taken Barry to make cookies with her boys. Diana felt she'd made excellent progress on the illustrations for a new children's book by Elsie Kenner for Brenner Publishing. She was a writer with a very vivid imagination. Diana quickly transposed her nursery characters from the verbal to the pictorial, dressing them in kaleidoscopic colors.

Diana wore an old green stain-riddled smock over trim straight-leg jeans and a white V-neck pullover. Her honey-colored hair was swept away from her face, tied back with a ribbon. Her complexion was smooth and clean with only a soft shade of lipstick enhancing her mouth. The pink tip of her tongue expressed her intense concentration as she applied newly mixed oils to the canvas.

She frowned in annoyance at the first peal of the doorbell. Thinking it must be Marty with Barry, she almost yelled "Come in," before realizing that Marty would have just knocked lightly a couple of times and pushed the door open. Irritated at the intrusion during her working hours and impatient at the caller's insistent ring, she called out, "Just a minute."

Diana dropped the smock in a chair and took a careless swipe at wiping her hands. She brushed back her hair, succeeding only in smudging her face with a dab of paint. It smeared even more as she tried to wipe it with the paint-stained cloth. The stray lock of hair remained unconfined, angering her even further.

"Blast it anyway," she murmured under her breath.

Little knowing how much her life was about to be disrupted, Diana yanked open the door.

Her annoyance was quickly replaced by a frown as Diana tried to recall where she'd seen the face before. A feeling of foreboding joined the frown as a flashback recalled an unpleasant memory. The man was dressed this time in a three-piece business suit instead of a . . . towel!

Startled she stared at him, her eyes not accepting what they saw. It couldn't be him. But it was.

A tremor of fear shot through her before she was able to contain it. Too late to pretend she didn't know who he was, she took refuge in anger, her voice barely audible. "What do you want? You told me once to stay away from you. The same applies to you as well, Caleb Buchanan." In a strangled whisper, she added, "Get out . . . and stay out of my life!"

"Not before I get what I came after. I believe you have something that belongs to the Buchanans."

It took Diana only a second to realize he meant Barry. Her face blanched white before her anger returned. "There is nothing here that belongs to you. Nothing! I would suggest . . ."

"I would suggest you sit down."

Without waiting for an invitation, Caleb stepped into the room. Diana automatically backed away. She did as he suggested not because of his command, but because her knees felt ready to buckle. He leaned against the dining room table, his arms crossed authoritatively, watching closely to gauge her reaction to his next words.

"First of all, I know about your child. About Barry." He paused a moment, allowing her to digest this information before continuing. "I've seen him up close, close enough to know without a doubt he is a Buchanan. It's a fact that anyone, even a perfect stranger, would know if they saw us together. They would probably insist he was my son instead of my nephew!"

"How . . . ? When did you see him?" Diana asked, her voice a husky whisper.

"A few days ago. You were getting off the train in Ames Crossing. Three feet separated us. You were just on the other side of a pane of glass." His dark eyes watched her as she absorbed this, before he added, "I made inquiries. A few phone calls brought me here."

"A matter of circumstances then . . . bad luck on my part?"

"And a missed plane on mine." His eyes held hers, waiting, anticipating what she would say.

"Why couldn't you just leave it there? Forget what you saw. As you see for yourself, Barry has a comfortable home. Would you care to look around? There is plenty of good wholesome food, vitamins, educational toys—all the things a little boy could want, need . . ." Diana's voice was high-pitched.

"Enough. You'll have yourself upset. I've come for Barry."

"Oh, fantastic!" Her eyes were wide, intensely green, her voice snapping with sarcasm. "Did you expect to walk in here without so much as a by-your-leave, and count on me to turn him over? Really, it's laughable."

"No. You can come, too."

"That's supposed to appeal to me?" she said, trying

to control herself. "Am I supposed to be so impressed by the Buchanan empire I'll just fall all over myself to become part of it? As I said, it's laughable!"

"I didn't expect to have your overwhelming approval —at first. But let me tell you this, no expense will be spared to fight so that Barry can have his rightful name and inheritance. Need I remind you," he added, his dark eyes watchful, "I'm a very wealthy man!"

Suddenly Diana was afraid. An intense fear shot through her, one she could not shrug off. Surely this man couldn't take Barry, the law wouldn't allow it. This was his home. He was happy here. But even as she tried to reassure herself, her memory recounted newspaper stories she'd read of real nightmares . . . horror stories where children had been taken from happy homes and put in the care of strangers. The idea of Barry being taken away . . . he couldn't really take Barry away, could he?

"If it is the right to see Barry occasionally, I am sure we can come to some agreement. Arrangements could be made . . . I could even move closer to Hartford."

"Not occasionally. All the time!" Caleb's dark brown eyes never left her face as he watched her reaction. "Barry will be the Buchanan heir."

"He wouldn't need to be a part of it, yet. He's only a little boy, a baby!"

"But he still needs to grow up with a knowledge of his heritage. In short, he needs roots, acceptance, and pride in what he is—a Buchanan—in everything but fact, and that is easily remedied."

"Oh sure, there's an easy out to everything as you see it," Diana protested hotly. "But what about me, Caleb Buchanan? Where am I supposed to fit into this rosy picture you're painting? Or doesn't love count on your list of priorities for Barry?"

Caleb's eyes never left her face as he spoke. He waited to gauge her reaction as he said, "Of course, you'll come too . . . as Barry's mother, and my wife!"

Unable to believe what she had heard, Diana stared at him. Marry him! The last person on earth she'd ever marry would be Caleb Buchanan!

Some of the incredible disbelief on her face must have seeped through to him. He said, with sardonic amusement, "You heard correctly."

"You've taken leave of your senses if you think I'd ever even consider marriage to you."

"But you will. . . ."

"Never . . . ever!" Diana protested. Standing up, she planted her hands on her hips, emphasizing how she regarded marriage to him.

"Don't make too hasty a decision. I agree with you that connubial bliss is a highly overrated state. But our marriage wouldn't be anything like the usual. Merely a home for Barry."

"He has a home. Here with me."

His voice was threatening as he turned to leave, "Remember, you were forewarned."

"Wait . . . please. This is moving too fast. I can't think straight." Her voice was shaky with fear as she tried unsuccessfully to keep it steady. "You wouldn't really try to take him away from me? Even you wouldn't be that cruel."

"Are you prepared to chance it?" he asked boldly, his brown eyes intense as he watched her. "As I said, you have two choices. Either you come willingly as my wife or we will fight for Barry's custody in a court of law."

Dismayed, she stared at him. Suddenly, in a matter of minutes, her life had become a labyrinth of indecision, a tangled complexity with both choices at cross purposes with her well-ordered existence. Trembling visibly, she turned away to stare bleakly out the window. The scene was unchanged in the bright April sunshine. It was still beautiful and peaceful, the scene in contrast with the turmoil going on within her.

What could she do? What choices were there? Terrified at what the outcome of a court battle might be, she knew she couldn't possibly chance it. She didn't have Caleb's influence, money, or power!

Inconceivable though it was, Diana knew what she had to do. Marry him! She actually had to give up her freedom and independence to become Mrs. Caleb Buchanan. She squared her shoulders. One thing she would not do was let him know what it cost her to make this frightening decision, committing herself to a life of such uncertainty.

Turning, she met his gaze unflinchingly, amazed at how well she carried it off with all the quaking inside her. He studied her, an eyebrow quirked, as she said vehemently, "For what it's worth, I'll marry you. But I swear you'll be the one who's going to regret what you're making me do against my will."

"Regret it? It's doubtful. Are you planning to take certain measures to insure I end up lamenting our marriage, making you do this, as you say, against your will?" His cool gaze was watchful.

"What a good idea!"

"Don't start anything you're not prepared to finish."

She liked a challenge. He scarcely frightened her with his dire warnings. She'd find his Achilles heel, like he'd found hers—Barry. Even the mighty Caleb Buchanan had a vulnerable spot under that calloused hide of his. She'd find it.

Watching him closely to gauge his reaction to this statement, she said, "Since you walked in that door, you've been delivering the ultimatums. Now I have one of my own. There is one item we haven't discussed yet and in this there will be no choice. This marriage will be strictly board only—*not bed and board*. Am I understood?"

Try as she might Diana couldn't keep the color from creeping into her face as she met and held the sardonic amusement in his eyes. The look continued, her own eyes a deep green under his scrutiny.

"As a normal adult male, I hope you don't have any objections to my finding companionship elsewhere?" he asked, the amusement in his voice causing her color to heighten even more.

As nonchalantly as possible, she said, "Of course. And you will allow me the same discreet freedom."

She turned away, unable to stand the dark probe any longer.

It was with profound amazement that she suddenly felt herself spun around by two powerful hands on her shoulders, his grip hard, his voice no longer amused as he spat, *"Never!"*

She couldn't help but recoil under the dark fury. Caleb gave her a rough shake. Transfixed by the vehement look in his eyes, Diana could sense the barely controlled anger in his hands.

"Never," he repeated. "If it becomes necessary to have a man in your bed, it will be *me!* You are talking to a different brother now. I am not so easily taken in as Barrett was. . . ."

". . . and as I am such a shallow, two-faced bride, you'd better guard me well. I'd love to make a complete fool of you."

His face was only inches from her own as they glared at each other. She couldn't actually believe she'd dared to say what she had. Diana expected this statement to make him even more furious, but suddenly the harshness left him as he saw through her scheme. She'd deliberately baited him, intentionally wished he'd act like an uncouth boor. He was on the brink of deciding that it was impossible to marry this green-eyed witch.

"I wouldn't advise you to continue in this vein. I can take whatever you can dish out, sweetheart, and more. But don't plan on making a buffoon of me," he advised. "I am not a submissive boy. Barrett had a lot of very endearing qualities, mainly a naturally trusting nature. He was without a doubt totally susceptible to a bewitchingly beautiful charmer like yourself. . . ."

". . . whereas I wouldn't be able to work any of my wiles on you?" she said, giving him a saccharine-sweet smile.

"Oh, did I say that?" he said, with a wicked grin, allowing his eyes to slide boldly in their appraisal. "Be prepared if you decide to try it. The outcome might be different than you envision. Diana, the Huntress, might become the prey. As my wife your conduct must be above reproach."

His wife!

With all this verbal sparring she'd forgotten why he'd come, what she'd agreed to. Now it all came rushing back, as she heard him say, "A week from Monday. I'll take care of all the details. You'll have only to arrange the necessary blood tests on your side. You've ten days to get used to the idea."

"A lifetime wouldn't be long enough!" she said scornfully.

"Monday, a week. Till then . . . I'll be in touch." He paused at the door. "Don't think you can disappear, either. You wouldn't have a prayer of a chance. I'd find you. After suing for custody and getting Barry, I'd wring your beautiful little neck!"

With this he closed the door firmly behind him, and Diana was alone.

* * *

As soon as he was gone, Diana felt an overwhelming desire to cry. She never cried, and had always managed to handle what fate handed her way without any trouble. Surely she'd find some way out of this dilemma. Slowly she sank into an overstuffed chair, which was how Marty found her minutes later when she came to return Barry.

"He's eaten, though not much after all the cookie dough," Marty said, eyeing Diana with a concerned air. "He's nodding off and should be ready for a nap without much prompting."

Standing up, Diana took him from Marty, hugging Barry close, her fear conveyed by the gesture.

Barry pushed against her saying, "Too tight . . . hold Barry too tight."

Diana loosened her grip, kissed his cheek, and laid him in his crib.

Moments later, Diana returned to the living room, a worried frown knitting her brow. Her eyes met the interested gaze of her friend. Marty might have been curious about Diana's past but she'd never even hinted about wanting to know. Diana suddenly felt the need to unburden her problem on Marty's shoulders. She felt she'd crack under the strain if she didn't have someone else's opinion. Was marriage to Caleb Buchanan her only out?

"You're curious?" she asked, ". . . about who *he* is?"

"Yes, if you wish to tell me," Marty answered. "I wondered when I directed him to your house if I had done the right thing. It didn't take much imagination to know he and Barry are related. With that dark scowl on his face when I came to the door," she shook her head as she recalled the look, "I knew he wouldn't have taken no for an answer."

"You're oh-so-right there," Diana said cynically. *"No*

36

is unacceptable in his vocabulary. He is as immovable as I've been led to believe."

"He isn't Barry's father?" Marty questioned.

"Good heavens, no! Though I can see how you came to that conclusion. No, Caleb Buchanan is his uncle, and contrary to what you've guessed, I am not Barry's mother . . . I'm his aunt!" Seeing the shocked surprised look on Marty's face, she added, "Perhaps I should start at the beginning—five years ago."

"If you're sure."

"I'm sure."

Chapter Four

Deanna and Diana had had a rather conventional upbringing in the small Connecticut town of Sharon. Their artistic inclinations were a heritage from two gifted parents. John Lacklain managed a small professional art gallery and was a very accomplished artist in his own right. His wife, Helen, a talented cellist, also ran a gift shop adjacent to the gallery. Both businesses catered to the summer tourists; the art gallery was full of paintings by young, talented artists in the area, while Helen's specialty was the local arts and crafts trade. Helen was also an authority on Colonial American antiques, and a portion of the shop had been set aside for the pewter, ironstone, and brass pots every visitor insisted on taking home.

The sisters, though very different in temperament as well as physical appearance, had nonetheless always been unusually close. Deanna, older by two years, was quieter and more circumspect. Small and dark-headed, she resembled her mother's side of the family. She was a good listener, more apt to be in the audience showing her appreciation of good music or watching the excellent summer stock plays Sharon was noted for. It was Diana who was the one calming butterflies backstage in anticipation of the next scene in which she had a part.

Diana had shown a growing talent as a fledgling actress and as an artist as well, since she'd sold her first sketch at the tender age of six in her father's art gallery. Diana more closely resembled the Nordic ancestry of her paternal grandmother. Tall and long-legged, she'd been given the nickname of "Ladder" around the age of twelve when she'd shot past the rest of her class in school. Somehow, she'd managed to come together in a rather attractive package. Her youthful gangliness had been transformed into a stunning figure, with full-breasted, almost Junoesque proportions, and she'd learned to carry her height gracefully. Most of the time she was unconscious of her beauty, and she considered her honey-colored hair and shapely legs her best assets.

Deanna, at twenty, had completed her first year of college on a music scholarship, and eighteen-year-old Diana had just finished high school, when their parents were killed in a car crash. Suddenly the two of them found themselves alone. It had been a frightening time.

Their future college plans were squashed under the more tangible need to earn a living. A close friend of their father's helped Diana find work with an insurance company in Hartford; it was a nationally known firm, one of several the city was famous for. It helped having the connection. Eighteen years of age and no experience were not the best credentials for finding a good job. In the evenings she was able to complete art courses at night school.

Deanna had obtained employment at Buchanan's Antiques and Imports Limited, one of the oldest and best-managed family firms in the business. While not as famous as Sotheby Park Bernet or Christie's, Buchanan's was very capably and competently directed by Caleb Buchanan, grandson of the founder. The business had been on the brink of bankruptcy because of the haphazard leadership of his alcoholic father when Caleb had taken charge of Buchanan's at the age of twenty-three. Now, eight years later, he had totally changed the outlook and the balance sheet of the company.

He'd developed a network of qualified experts worldwide, whom he had personally trained to ferret out the especially scarce piece, the truly rare find. He often traveled to London or the Continent himself, if it meant locating a particular painting or art object for a client. He was a hawk who rarely came back without its prey. Caleb Buchanan had seen the forthcoming trend toward collecting specific period pieces before it manifested itself and everyone was rushing to cash in on the idea. It was that foresight that enabled him to build the company far beyond his grandfather's dreams.

Barrett Buchanan was younger than Caleb by four years. More likable, less exacting than his brother, he was more willing to give someone a second chance if something did happen to get damaged or broken. Barrett handled the cataloging, warehousing, auctions, and security. Each brother had his own areas of concern, and they seldom met.

When Barrett began working on a book he'd always wanted to write on antiques—a layman's introduction to building a priceless collection—he needed someone to help with the cataloging and typing. Deanna had been at Buchanan's almost a year. She had a sizable knowledge of antiques, both from her work there and from her mother's shop. Knowing this, Barrett had pulled Deanna from the typing pool to help with the manuscript.

The attraction between Barrett and Deanna evolved slowly; it was a mutual need for companionship, a common ground of similar likes and dislikes. The feelings that developed into love were kept on a friendship basis long after they both were aware of the changes.

Barrett was a married man. No matter how unhappily; it didn't change the fact that he *was* married.

Diana first became uneasy about the relationship when her sister told her that Barrett wanted to move the writing to Woodledge, a weekend estate on several heavily wooded acres. It had been owned by the Buchanan family for three generations. It was an hour's drive from Hartford, and Barrett felt they should stay over several days at a stretch. They would be well chaperoned, Dee had reassured Diana; an older caretaker and his wife lived there year round. The book was progressing so nicely that without the interruptions and distractions of the office, they would finish the job more quickly.

Days became weeks and Diana again voiced her concern. This time Deanna became upset over her sister's "nagging." Angry words were exchanged, a rare occurrence between them. Diana felt terrible about the rift.

Burdened with guilt, Deanna had finally broken down and admitted to her sister that she was in love with Barrett Buchanan, and that, recently, she had found out that he felt the same way about her.

"We were so afraid his wife might find out—" Deanna's voice shook with emotion, pleading for understanding, "—or Caleb, his brother. We had to keep it to ourselves. Barry is going to live in New Haven for a while—where Buchanan's Import office is located. We thought it best not to see each other until Irene agreed to talk about a divorce."

During the next months they communicated by letter. Those missives were the only occasion of joy in Dee's life. October, November, December passed. Diana watched her sister become a slight shadow of herself, unhappiness etched in her pretty face. It was mid-March when Diana learned that Deanna was expecting Barrett's child.

Diana could vividly remember her shock, and could still picture the two of them, Barrett's arm protectively around Dee, their hands tightly clasped together. They were going away if Irene again refused to give Barrett a divorce. Although she tried not to stand in judgment, Diana felt he must have taken advantage of Dee. She was such a shy, sweet innocent. But Deanna would hear none of it.

"Di, be fair. I knew long ago how strong the attraction was. At first, I thought it was all on my side. I couldn't believe it when Barry confessed he felt the same. Even when I knew, I resigned myself that nothing could come of it until he was free. I knew it could be a long time, *if ever*. We happened to end up in a situation which we weren't able to say no to . . . no, let me tell her," Deanna added, shaking her head when Barrett would have interrupted.

"I made the mistake of driving out to Woodledge, where we'd spent so many happy hours," Deanna continued. "Long walks in the cold autumn air, pretending as we crunched through the leaves that we were on our way home, to *our* home. I didn't know he'd come for the weekend from New Haven. . . ."

". . . or that when I'd arrived in Hartford," Barrett insisted, "I'd found Irene on one of her endless 'shopping sprees' to New York. I had intended to tell her I'd find my own grounds for a divorce and also that Caleb should at last know the truth about the farce we called a marriage. When she wasn't home, out of loneliness I drove to the retreat—to Woodledge—where I'd found the only happiness I'd had in years. There, huddled in her old car, was Dee, my joy, half-frozen and as miserable as I."

Suddenly Diana remembered an incident right after

Christmas that had been totally out of character for her sister. She'd left word at Diana's office that she'd gone to New York to see a musical with friends. The message had been vague. Later, Dee had left another message with the landlady that they'd become snowbound and had to stay another night. Now, she knew Deanna had lied.

Deanna realized what Diana was thinking. She said softly, her blue eyes full of pain, hating the confession she must make, "It was the one time I ever lied to you, Di. The wrongfulness of it wasn't considered—not then. I was the one who made the call. Barry tried to stop me. But I love him so—that's my only excuse. I wanted to pretend he was mine, even for one snow-bound weekend."

Barrett had then tried to explain about the preceding years, wanting Diana to completely understand that Dee wasn't responsible for the breakdown of his marriage. It had been a sham from the beginning.

Diana had liked Barrett. She'd sensed his sincerity as he tried to be as fair as possible in relating the circumstances surrounding his engagement and eventual marriage to Irene Baxter. Barrett had taken most of the blame upon himself. But, in trying to be completely unbiased, he nonetheless gave Diana a very unfavorable impression of Caleb Buchanan. Caleb enjoyed his freedom. Although he hadn't any desire to forfeit his single status, he wasn't averse to Barrett's losing his!

The picture Diana got of Caleb was that of a playboy with a string of more-than-willing women at his beck and call, while Barrett seemed to be the victim of his brother's maneuvering. One of them should marry, produce an heir, and Caleb much preferred the "marrying Buchanan" to be his brother, not himself. Even a heated argument on the eve of Barrett's wedding had ended with Caleb the eventual victor.

"I stomped out of the room. 'Marry her yourself,' I told him," Barrett related to Diana. "The results were the same. Hours later, I came back and allowed Caleb to ply me with black coffee, and soberly conceded to his stronger influence and his judgment that matters 'would eventually work themselves out.' You can't make a commitment of that magnitude having the doubts I had. I should have been strong enough to make him realize it."

From the honeymoon on it had been a disaster!

Irene's main interest in life seemed to be how big a wardrobe she could acquire. They had spent their honeymoon in Paris, going from one dress salon to another. Finally, disgusted, Barrett had left and had flown home without Irene.

When Irene returned a few days later, the pattern for the rest of their life together was set. She went straight to Caleb, all in tears, with some tale about Barrett's callous initiation of their marriage leaving her completely cold and unresponsive, his uncivilized behavior having been so totally unexpected. Irene confessed that she'd gone on an extravagant spending spree to indulge herself after their quarrels.

Caleb's unquestioning belief in the story disgusted Barrett so much that he took the easy out and did nothing. "It was stupid of me to let Irene get away with it. But quite frankly, I didn't even care."

Both Diana's and Marty's thoughts were riveted on the past as they stared at one another, reliving the pain of her sister's lost love. The coffee had long ago gone cold in their cups as Diana added, "After that there isn't much to tell, Marty." Unable to hide the sadness in her voice, Diana stated, "It was a month later, in mid-April, when Barrett was killed. His car had plunged off a steep embankment. Irene was in the car with him. In fact, there was some question that she might have been driving. She ended up in a wheelchair, unable to walk."

"Poor Deanna was beside herself with grief," Diana went on. "The only thing that helped at all was the coming baby."

Then Diana told Marty about the first meeting at Woodledge with Caleb Buchanan when she'd gone after Dee's letters, adding, "We probably would have left Hartford immediately after that awful night, except the doctor had told Deanna she must stay in bed or risk losing the baby."

"When we finally did leave, it was just Barry and myself." Again the sadness permeated her voice as Diana added, "Dee made me promise that I'd move away from Hartford and Caleb Buchanan if anything happened to her. It was as if she had a premonition. She was afraid of him, that if he ever found out about Barry he would try to get him. How right she was!" she finished vehemently.

"Marty," she asked, "can you think of any other answer to this predicament without risking a custody suit? If he found out the true relationship—that I am Barry's aunt instead of his mother—it would be a powerful weapon. Do I actually have no other choice but to marry him?"

"I guess you *could* marry someone else!"

"But I don't know anyone else. Wait a minute," she ventured. "Steve! Hum . . . I wonder? Would it work? All I'd have to do is let Caleb *think* I'm marrying someone else. Steve would be willing to help, I'm sure."

"Steve?" Marty asked. "He's the one from Boston, the one who has been calling since you got back?"

Diana didn't have a phone so when an occasional need arose, she used Marty and Jeff's. Marty was aware that a man had called several times since Diana's return from Boston.

"That's right. He's coming up this weekend."

"But you hardly know him. You couldn't ask him to be part of some scheme!" Marty's voice was full of doubt.

"I hardly know Caleb Buchanan either, but it didn't stop him from causing trouble in my life. Of the two choices I prefer Steve Brenner. He's the first person I've enjoyed myself with enough to want to repeat the evening in a long time."

"But how would you . . . ?"

"Ask him? Leave it to me. It shouldn't be too hard." Thinking out loud she continued, "It would just be a temporary engagement."

"I have a distinct feeling," Marty injected, "that Caleb won't like it."

"You're right there, but Caleb won't know till it's fact. Then he can't do anything about it. Maybe you'd better not tell any of this to Jeff until we see how things work out."

"If they do!" Marty said, her voice once again full of doubt. "The first thing is getting Steve's approval. How will you . . . ?"

"I can handle it," Diana said confidently, more confidently than she felt at the moment.

Steve arrived the next evening in a cloud of dust. Undoubtedly he had burned up the asphalt between Boston and Ames Crossing in his sports car. Full of his usual enthusiasm, he didn't seem to notice Diana's nervousness and preoccupation or her less than eager answers to his questions.

He admired the old-fashioned flavor of the farm-house and noticed how she'd encouraged it with the decor. Jeff had nailed up the old hand-hewn barn wood in a wainscoting effect, and Marty had helped hang the washable print wallpaper above it. The addition of a few scatter rugs on the hardwood floors, some old refinished pieces of furniture and black iron pots full of greenery all added to the homey atmosphere. Steve's approval of how she'd arranged the old farmhouse made Diana realize the resentment she would have over leaving it.

Barry was napping at Marty's so Diana would have a chance to talk to Steve alone. She needed to see if he was receptive to the idea of helping her with the quandary she found herself involved in.

Steve had been there nearly two hours before Diana had enough nerve to broach the subject, but instead of her carefully rehearsed speech, she blurted out, "Steve, I'm in an awful predicament. I need to be engaged to someone. Would you consider it?"

Never would Diana forget the funny look on his face before his mouth broke into a wide, crooked grin and he said with disbelief, "I must be getting senile. The old ears are completely shot. I could have sworn you said you wanted to marry me!" Puzzled he added, "You're in love with me. No, of course, you're not," he said, answering his own question. "You're not some flighty girl who falls in love with every man she dates."

"I'm not in love with *anyone,*" Diana stated vehemently.

"Then why the proposal?" His blue eyes were suddenly watchful. "A rush to the altar might raise an eyebrow or two. You aren't pregnant?"

"No, there isn't any possibility of that." Her face felt warm under his thoughtful look.

Steve's sense of humor returned. "If marrying me would help, I suppose I could cope."

"It wouldn't have to be a marriage. An engagement would do. Maybe I should explain."

Steve agreed. "It would probably be a good idea."

As briefly as possible Diana told him. "It has to do with a little boy. He might be taken from me if I become involved in a custody suit with his uncle. The uncle thinks we should marry, to give the child his rightful name. I don't want to marry him or anyone— but *especially not him.* Barry's uncle is an egotistical, opinionated bore. He'd make my life miserable if I married him. All I need is a reprieve. Given a few months, maybe I can convince him to see the light. Someone else's ring on my finger should make him realize I don't want to marry him!"

"This little boy . . . who is he?"

"I didn't give birth to him, but he's been mine since he was born."

It was the only explanation she offered.

Steve watched her closely, sensing her hesitation, but he didn't ask for any further details. But he did ask thoughtfully, "What if I wanted to continue the engagement to its natural conclusion? What then? You know I wouldn't be here unless I had the idea of getting better acquainted."

"I like you, too," Diana said emphasizing the word *like*. "If the engagement continued into marriage, it would have to be something we both wanted. In my twenty-three years I haven't had the best of experiences where men are concerned.

"I told you about the wager over me . . . only I didn't tell you *all* of it. One night after rehearsals I heard the two of them talking, and essentially the bet was 'who could bed the leading lady first'! I never even told my sister. I was too embarrassed. Neither one . . ."

"It goes without saying, Diana," Steve injected, "neither one won the bet!"

Diana thanked him with a look, her eyes still unable to hide the hurt and humiliation she'd endured. "There have been other incidents which left me a little bruised. The last one happened just before I moved from Hartford, and it swore me off men."

"I was working at an insurance firm there and one of the company executives was paying me some marked attention. I managed to avoid him most of the time, but once he outmaneuvered me. He took me to lunch, where he confided his marriage was on the rocks. The funny part was I saw the pass and avoided him like the plague. A few nights later at a company party his wife reproved me about asking him to lunch. She came at me with talons exposed. Her husband stood there and let her tear my reputation to shreds.

"Even the date I'd gone to the party with saw me in a different light. He was all hands when he took me home. I was glad for an excuse to leave Hartford after that lovely evening. I've avoided the male sex since then."

The hand that was resting on the back of the sofa touched her shoulder. Steve said gravely, "Diana, what I think you need is a friend . . . a male friend. We aren't all rotten, you know."

She answered his smile with one of her own, saying, "I know, but I'm not a very good judge of character. I'd like you to be my friend, Steve. It's exactly what I need."

"Affectionate friends," he corrected. "Okay?"

"Okay," she echoed, allowing him to pull her close. Moments later, he said with his usual boyish enthusiasm, "Come on, let's go eat. That barbecue Jeff and Marty promised should be about ready, and I'm starved. Besides I think it's about time I met your son."

It was an enjoyable weekend. Jeff and Marty had asked Steve to stay with them and by the time Sunday morning had rolled around Steve was accepted by both the Burnsides. Even Barry, who was cautious with his friendships, had warmed under Steve's charm.

They'd gone on a picnic the day before and when the day was over Barry had permitted Steve to carry him back to the car without much ado. Chewing thoughtfully on his finger, Barry had watched this strange man with solemn brown eyes, checking every once in a while to make sure his "Dee-dee"—his nickname for Diana —was following close behind.

Tired, a bit dust-covered and sunburned, Diana was never the less a little more relaxed about the engagement. "It just might work."

Even doubtful Marty voiced her opinion. She commented how likable Steve was and added, "I hope you'll fall in love and live happily ever after!"

Jeff had clapped Steve on the back when Steve mentioned he'd be back next weekend with a ring for Diana's finger. Unaware it was anything but a normal engagement, Jeff knew nothing of Caleb Buchanan or the fact that Diana was supposed to marry him. And it was Jeff who allowed Caleb to find out about Steve Brenner and squash their "engagement" before it even got off the ground.

Later, Diana pieced together the details enough to know what had happened.

Caleb had called at the beginning of the week, mainly to let Diana know the details concerning their wedding, which was to take place the following Monday.

Jeff answered the phone. The voice on the other end asked for Diana, adding, "This is her fiancé."

"Good morning, Steve. Diana hasn't come over yet this morning. Dreaming of wedding bells, no doubt."

"No doubt," the voice on the line replied tersely, very interested in this conversation.

"I'll have her call," Jeff told him. "Let's see, here's your name and number jotted on the calendar." Repeating it out loud he said, "Diana has even written down your work number, too. 'Brenner Publishing'," he read and then added the phone number. "Correct?"

"Uhuh," was the deep reply. The voice added, "But you needn't tell her I called. I'd like to surprise her. What time do you think she'll be over?"

"She usually does the bookkeeping immediately after lunch, while Barry is napping," Jeff answered. "Sure you don't want me to have her call?"

"No, I like surprises. I'll call back then," was the curt reply. Caleb hung up.

Diana had been working just a few minutes when the phone rang. She swallowed as she recognized Caleb's deep resonant voice. "Diana, I thought we understood each other when I left there. I told you what I'd do if you tried anything."

"What do you mean?" she asked, apprehensive, a tingling sensation traveling along her spine.

"Steven Brenner!"

She gasped before she could control it. How in the world had he found out? Trembling, she felt as if doomsday had arrived. She swallowed, the inside of her mouth as dry as a dust bowl. Her voice sounded husky when she was finally able to speak. "You know," she whispered. "But how? You couldn't possibly."

"I told you what I'd do! Now you'll see I'm a man of my word!"

"I don't know how you found out. I admit it was a

stupid idea. But I was desperate, and desperate people take desperate measures. Caleb, I don't want to marry you." Diana pounded her fist on the desk, wishing it was his chest she was beating on!

"I'm not crazy about the idea either, but we will marry. It's either that or a custody suit," Caleb threatened. "Now you decide which it's to be."

"I can't think now. I'll call you back later." She didn't give him a chance to reply and hurriedly hung up the phone.

She was at a stalemate with no way out. Diana felt a cold tightness in the pit of her stomach. Every way she turned Caleb Buchanan was there, interfering in her life.

She buried her face in her hands, fighting back tears of frustration. Honestly, she thought, *I can't believe my luck—all bad!* How in the world had he found out? It was a fantastic stroke of good luck for Caleb.

Diana pushed the button on the intercom and spoke into the receiver. "Marty, could you keep an eye on Barry for me? I'd like to go for a walk. There's a problem I need to sort out."

At Marty's affirmative reply, Diana pulled on her windbreaker and slipped out the side door. She hurried down the rutted path that ran along a stone-walled field. She knew where she was headed—her Place of Rocks, she'd named it. It was an outcropping of boulders too numerous to bother with discarding, so the neighboring farmer had just plowed around them. Diana had gone there on occasion when she was troubled.

Once there she heaved up against one of the largest rocks and gave vent to the long held-back anger. Incredibly, her angry thoughts were leveled at her sister. *Why did you have to die and leave me to make all these decisions on my own concerning Barry? Why didn't you fight? Oh, Dee, Dee, what will I do if I lose him?*

After several minutes of voicing her frustration, agonizing over the situation, Diana began to feel guilty over the berating angle of her thoughts. She had loved her sister dearly. They'd been very close, so close that all during Deanna's pregnancy Diana had begun to see that Deanna had no will to live in a world without Barrett. She had tried to make her see that their child needed her, but, soon after Barry's birth, Deanna had quietly slipped away.

Because circumstances precluded taking out anger on someone she loved, Diana turned her thoughts to the one person she felt was responsible for her present predicament. Caleb Buchanan. She pounded her fist against her blue-jean-clad leg. She'd marry him; there didn't seem to be any choice in the matter, but she intended to make him pay and pay and pay! She didn't give in to the tears that were just below the surface, fighting them as she always did, but in their place was a searing anger, a burning desire for restitution for being forced into an unwilling marriage!

She waited until the next morning to call him. *Let him stew,* she rationalized.

"Okay, I'll phone Steve and call it off. It seems I don't have another choice," she said angrily when she had him on the phone.

"Don't think you can carry on with him later behind my back. I've already told you my sentiments on that. I won't be made a fool of."

"You can't dictate who my friends are!"

"Friends!" he jeered. "By the time it's an engagement, lovers would be more like it."

"Believe what you want. You will anyway."

"Barrett may have been easily swayed, but you'll answer to me, once we are man and wife."

"You won't get your way about everything."

"Anything to make friction," he commented.

"Anything, darling," she echoed with sugary sweetness and hung up. "Why me?" she cried.

It wasn't easy finding the nerve to call Steve, especially since she'd started the whole mess in the first place. But it was better not to put it off. A delay wouldn't make it any easier.

"I'm afraid our engagement didn't fool him at all, Steve. He's already found out."

"The uncle?" he asked.

"Yes. I don't know how, but he did."

"Diana, you needn't be afraid. He can't force you."

"That's where you're wrong. I won't risk a custody suit over Barry." A cold shiver shot through her body. She didn't want to think about the possibility of losing Barry.

"If it's money maybe I could help. My grandmother left me a tidy little sum."

"No. It would be a waste. Caleb Buchanan is not a loser!"

"Caleb Buchanan! The owner of Buchanan Imports? Is he the uncle? No wonder you're scared!"

"You know him?" Diana asked.

"Not well. I've met him a couple of times. But my mother thinks he can do no wrong. Remember her art gallery that she showed you?"

"A beautiful collection," Diana commented.

"Well, Caleb Buchanan is the one who started her on French Impressionist paintings. She's done so well monetarily that Dad finally quit calling it 'her little hobby.' Buchanan's has a well-deserved reputation. It was Caleb who built his grandfather's business into one of the biggest brokerage houses for art and antiques in the country," he finished.

"Well, I'm unimpressed!" she scoffed. "I wish I'd never heard of Buchanan's, or its owner."

"He also has quite a reputation with women. You've landed one of the biggest fish in the sea."

"I'd just as soon throw him back! Are you trying to sell me on Caleb Buchanan?" she asked. "You'll have a good job of it!"

"I was just trying to make you realize what you're letting yourself in for. You still intend to marry him?"

"Believe me, if I had a choice, the last person I'd marry would be him!"

Chapter Five

Things were not going well. Then again, had she expected her wedding day to be anything but the "black day" it was turning out to be? Marriage to Caleb Buchanan was not the high point of her life.

The doorbell rang and there was Caleb, two hours early. Diana gave him an angry glance before she stepped aside to allow him in. "Afraid I'd run away?" she snapped, irritated. She'd been dreading this moment all day.

His eyes held a gleam of amusement. "If anyone should run it ought to be me! I have the decided feeling you're going to be nothing but a big disruption in a once well-ordered life."

"I'll do my best," she promised.

"I'm sure you will."

While this exchange was going on Barry had toddled out of his room and stood, watching his uncle with dark, solemn eyes. When Caleb noticed him, he walked over and stooped down, offering Barry an outstretched hand. "I think it's about time we got acquainted, young man."

Barry glanced first at the hand, then at the tall, broad-shouldered man, before he puckered his face and began crying very loudly.

Good, Diana thought, with a triumphant smile in

Caleb's direction. *Barry doesn't like him either.* She enjoyed her small victory as she picked Barry up and took him into the bedroom to finish packing a few remaining items. Barry had been fretful and restless, sleeping little during naptime. Now a total stranger had invaded his domain.

She stuffed the dress she'd been going to wear into the bag, too. What difference did it make if she wore blue jeans? This wasn't any conventional wedding. It was nonsense to pretend any different. She ran a brush through her hair, not even bothering with lipstick. She didn't want Caleb to think she was enjoying this!

When she returned to the living room Caleb glanced meaningfully at the blue jeans before merely shrugging his broad shoulders. He was dressed in an immaculate light tan suit, custom-tailored to his well-built body. He picked up the suitcases and waited for her to precede him out the door. Once outside he helped her into a silver-blue Mercedes coupe that had a brand new sticker in the window. Evidently whenever one of his cars broke down he just bought a new one!

With only a benchlike seat behind the bucket seats Diana had doubts about where she'd lay Barry if naptime finally became a necessity. He wasn't the best traveler, especially when he wasn't feeling well. She thought he was teething.

As she glanced at Marty and Jeff's house, Diana felt a tightness in her throat. They'd already said their good-byes and it hadn't been easy. Marty had helped fill the void created by Deanna's death, and though they'd promised to keep in touch, it wouldn't be the same, and both of them were aware of it as they'd hugged each other that morning. They'd been hard pressed to keep from crying, especially when Ricky and Joey kept asking so many questions.

"Why do you have to go away? It's no fun without

Barry to play with. Why do you have to go to 'Nedicut'? Why do you have to get married, anyway?"

And Marty—good solid New England stock, the salt of the earth, she and Diana had been great friends. It had been so easy to call on her, even in the middle of the night, if some problem cropped up she didn't know how to handle. Diana was an inexperienced mother and Marty's advice had been reliable.

Caleb had arranged for them to be married by a Justice of the Peace in the small Vermont border town of Whitingham. It would take only a few minutes for the ceremony, he'd said. *A few minutes,* Diana thought scornfully, *to ruin my life.*

The miles seemed to fly by. Caleb was a competent driver, but the grim set to his mouth and his long fingers gripping the wheel made Diana think he wasn't too happy about this marriage either.

Barry was watchful, his eyes on his uncle with sober concern, although there were no more outbursts of crying or temper. The restrainer chair held him up high enough to allow him to see out and he was content for the moment. The numbers on the road signs stating the miles to Whitingham kept getting smaller and smaller.

Jonathan P. Whitingham, Justice of the Peace, the sign on the mailbox said.

Caleb had been correct when he had said the ceremony would only take a few minutes, but Diana was sure their marriage would be the topic of gossip for weeks to come in the small town. It was undoubtedly the most unorthodox ceremony Jonathan P. Whitingham had ever performed—no sweet smell of orange blossoms or soft organ music, merely an occasional dark look, with a terse, "Hurry up," from Caleb injected now and then. The main thing Diana remembered about it was an insane desire to laugh!

The urge started when she got her first look at the minister and his wife. Both of them had been interrupted at what they'd been doing. The J.P. was dressed in an old sweater, a pair of baggy tweeds and dirt-covered tennis shoes—he'd been gardening, no doubt. His wife's arms were encrusted with dough—she must have been making a batch of bread. The J.P. and wife watched the proceedings with a puzzled expression on their faces. Every once in a while Diana would see a meaningful look pass between them, each peering over a pair of bifocal glasses at the other.

Barry became restless halfway through the ceremony and began to fuss. Diana tried to shift him to the other arm, but that arm was the one nearest Caleb. But this was a big mistake; the huge stranger was much too close and Barry began to cry again in earnest. Mrs. Whitingham offered to take the "wee lad," but she was an unknown, too. By the time she handed him back to Diana, Barry was up to full range on the decibel scale.

Then Caleb, with a curt "Here, give him to me," plucked him from Diana's arms. This action actually increased the volume, and if this was not enough, he planted a well-placed wallop on Barry's rear. All pandemonium broke loose. Barry, his arms outstretched, wanted only one person. "Dee-dee, Dee-dee," he screamed over and over again.

When she tried to take him back, Caleb glared down at her and said sharply, "Leave him be! Hurry up," he repeated to the Justice of the Peace. *Peace—a funny word to be bandied about,* Diana thought, *with all this racket going on.*

Suddenly she couldn't contain it any longer. She laughed! The laughter bubbled inside her throughout the rest of the ceremony. Caleb jabbed a gold band on her finger, scraping her knuckle in the process. This act was followed by the J.P.'s saying, "I now pronounce you man and wife. You can kiss the bride."

"Kiss her!" Caleb snapped. "That's not exactly what I feel like doing!" He stuffed a couple of large bills in the man's hand and roughly ushered his new family out the door.

The Whitinghams didn't wait till they were out of earshot to express their amazement. Diana and Caleb both heard them through an open window. "Well, I never! Did you see the child? Why he's the spitting image of his father. It's about time I'd say! And denim trousers at a wedding! I can't remember ever performing a ceremony where the bride and groom glared at each other the whole time!"

During this exchange Caleb handed Barry to Diana. By this time, Barry was hiccuping. Even a light swat was a very rare occurrence in his world, and it had somewhat sobered him.

She watched as Caleb shrugged out of his jacket and took off his tie before throwing them in the trunk of the car. Diana knew all hell would break loose if she teased him. But she couldn't help herself. She cooed at Caleb, his profile grim in the fading light as he set the car in motion. "Daddy must buy a bigger car for Mommy and baby. Babykins thinks Daddy should get a station wagon now that Daddy is a family man. Don't you think so, Daddy?"

The idea of Caleb driving one of those great "beached whales" set the laughter churning inside her despite the black look he gave her.

"Then Daddy can take Mommy and baby to the grocery store and the pediatrician and later to the P.T.A. Won't that be fun . . . hum?"

"Diana, I've had enough humor for one day!"

"Oh . . . Daddy's had a bad day, baby. Isn't that

sad? Poor, poor Daddy," Diana said, clicking her tongue.

But the baby wasn't listening—he'd gone to sleep. Diana lifted him into the back and strapped him into his car seat. He was so tired he never moved.

In a terse, angry voice, Diana heard Caleb say, "You think you're being so clever. I'm warning you, if you don't want me to stop this car, you'd better stop. Quite frankly I can't see what you find so amusing."

She commented drily, as she settled back in the seat, "There are things you don't understand."

"Try me."

Her eyes a deep green, she said, "Since the age of six I've wondered about my wedding day, but never in my wildest imagination was it anything like what just happened!"

"I'm glad it amused one of us."

"If you could have seen your face . . ." Diana was unable to finish the sentence. All the mirth made her sides ache.

"Very funny," he said sarcastically. But somewhere deep inside she heard a small inflection in his speech that told her he was finding some humor in all this, despite himself.

Pulling into a widened area beside the road, Caleb jeered, "I guess I'll have to think of a way to make you shut up. I think, Mrs. Buchanan, it is time to kiss the bride!"

"No!" She barely mouthed the word before his lips closed over hers, as he pulled her roughly into his arms. With a viselike grip he held her tightly, forcing her against his hard body, his hand tangled painfully in her hair. Wiggling her hands upward, she tried to push some room between them. He leaned away as if to accommodate her. In allowing the movement, he must have thought she wanted to touch him, to . . . *heavens,* she thought, *to caress him,* as the long-fingered hand at her back was moving warmly over her body.

She began to struggle, pushing at his chest, aware of the rapid beating of his heart against the palm of her hand. She was conscious also of the flaming awareness inside herself. She knew instinctively that he would be a good lover. Her body radiated a warmth, a hot sweetness that was becoming increasingly hard to resist.

She tried to speak, to make him stop, but parting her lips was a mistake. He took advantage of the opportunity she afforded him, tasting the warm recesses of her mouth with a lazy exploration. She began to shake, terrified of her own emotions, as his hand became more intimate, sliding around to cup the fullness of her breast, holding the weight of it experimentally in his palm.

He had to stop, must stop—the way to pay him back was not to become involved herself! The conflict between the two continued, he demanding a response, and she, trying unsuccessfully not to give it.

In the struggle he accidentally bumped the horn, which caused Barry to whimper in his sleep. She glared at Caleb as they broke apart.

"You'll wake Barry," she stated hotly.

"Actually it's you I was trying to awaken," he said significantly. "You still have an untouched look about you. But we both know that couldn't possibly be."

"No, not possibly, could it?" she said, then added, "You weren't supposed to do that. Lovemaking isn't part of our marriage."

"You asked for it."

Diana had no response. She clearly had baited him and gotten more than she had bargained for. "Just keep your distance," she said watching him warily for any possible resumption of the kissing.

"Okay, keep quiet and I'll think about it."

"Actually," she said as he started the car, "I really felt more like crying than laughing. The laughter was just an outlet for pent-up emotions. I never cry."

"I've heard it said that witches never do!"

She gave him a rueful smile. "Am I a witch?"

"Yes. A green-eyed witch, one who has come to practice her sorcery on me." Then he added, almost to himself, "I wonder if I could make you cry."

A slow steady drizzle began before they arrived in Hartford. Somehow the rain seemed appropriate. Although there was an absence of thunder and lightning, it was still a reminder of the night they had first met.

Conversation had long since lagged between them and the ensuing silence had not been a comfortable one. Each had his own thoughts, and if his were anything like her own, they weren't very flattering. She might be married to him, but she didn't have to like it, or pretend that she did!

Vaguely Diana recalled Deanna's mention of Caleb's home, noted for its opulent surroundings and unrivaled collection of antiques. Never would she forget her first glimpse of it—even in the fast approaching darkness it was impressive.

The estate, accessible only through a wrought iron gate and security checkpoint, was surrounded by a brick wall. It was in a secluded, exclusive area; the paved entrance was bordered by a long private drive lined with a dozen oak trees, giving it its name—Twelve Trees. It was a magnificent Georgian mansion, which Caleb's grandfather had restored to house his growing collection of priceless treasures. He'd cherished his hoard of antiques almost like they were children. Twelve Trees was the perfect setting once he'd returned it to its former grandeur.

Originally constructed by a wealthy landowner after the Revolutionary War, it boasted of being one of the most elegant establishments outside of England. It was a showplace, built to accommodate as many as twenty guests a night.

The back balcony of the house overlooked sweeping lawns and formal gardens, together with swimming pool, tennis courts, stables and even a lake for boating.

Caleb pulled up to the front entry. Stepping from the car he walked around to help Diana out of the car. Even though she was stiff from the long drive, she ignored the arm he offered. However, she allowed him to carry Barry, who protested only slightly at being moved.

If she'd been impressed by the outside, the rest of the house was breathtaking. The formal entry was spacious, expanding into the living area. A Sheraton sofa, in a gold and white brocade, accompanied the Chippendale settee and side chairs with their delicate, tapered legs. From the French rococo chandelier to the Persian and Kazak rugs that lined the hardwood floors, it all spelled one word—*Money*.

They were met by a gray-haired man Caleb called Sterns. The butler had a quiet dignity about him, and although it was hard to detect, there was an ever-so-slight change in his expression as Caleb introduced Diana as his wife. It clued her in to the fact that this marriage had never been mentioned before.

"Your wife, sir? May I offer my congratulations!"

"Congratulations aren't necessary," Caleb answered. "Would you see they have rooms, one for Diana and one for the boy."

"Next to yours, sir?"

"No, the east end of the upstairs hall will be fine."

"Very good. I'll have them readied immediately," Sterns replied, never letting on if this order seemed strange to him. As he turned to leave he remembered something. Although he spoke in a low voice Diana was near enough to overhear.

"The other Mrs. Buchanan arrived this afternoon. I put her in the downstairs suite because of her wheelchair. I hope that's all right, sir?"

"You know best, Sterns." Caleb didn't appear too happy over this latest development. A frown knitted his brow as he added, "I suppose I'd better go see what's up. How long will she be staying?"

"Indefinitely, I believe."

"I see."

Diana thought he didn't *see* at all, if the furrowed brow was any indication.

Sterns left to help with the luggage. When he was gone Caleb rang for someone to help with Barry. Turning to Diana he said, "I'll see you later. Something has come up."

Diana smiled sweetly, amusement in her voice and eyes. "Like another Mrs. Buchanan? Poor Caleb. Two in one day! It must be Barrett's wife." She added sarcastically, "I've heard she's a sweetheart, too!"

Caleb gave her a black look. It was probably all he dared. The arrival of another servant, a buxom young girl named Lottie, undoubtedly saved her from a scathing retort. With a wholesome freckled face, Lottie looked like she'd come straight from a farm. After introductions (she, too, had a note of surprise on her round face), Lottie took Barry saying, "Follow me, Mrs. Buchanan. I'll show you and the little boy to your rooms."

"If they need a tray, see to it, will you Lottie?" Caleb asked, as they turned to leave. "I've other things on my mind."

"We're fine. Barry won't wake up now before morning and I'm not the least bit hungry," Diana answered.

Although she could feel a hollowness in her stomach, the idea of eating made her feel slightly sick. She suddenly felt exhausted. "Go take care of your *other things,* Caleb. I'll manage."

Diana followed Lottie upstairs and into one of the most beautiful rooms she had ever seen. A huge cherrywood four-poster bed dominated it. A cable-stitched hand-knit spread covered the bed, while the canopy was draped with a crocheted curtain. There was also an Oxbow front highboy and a Kittinger writing desk. The wallpaper was a copy of an eighteenth-century stenciled design with the tiny flowers and leaves captured in sage green and creamy white. Hand-made champagne lace curtains covered the panels of the french windows and door.

The door opened onto a long, low balcony which stretched the length of the two-story structure. At each end of the balcony was a curved stairway that circled into the formal garden and pool area below.

Barry's room was next to hers and had been used by several generations of Buchanans as a nursery. It was full of antique baby furniture, which had already seen several Buchanans through babyhood—a carved cradle, a high-sided crib, and a rocking horse.

Lottie helped her undress Barry. He slept through the whole feat, never stirring at all as they tugged pajamas on his limp little body. With Barry going to bed so early in the car, he'd probably be up at the crack of dawn.

Once he was in the crib, Lottie said a little inquisitively, "When instructions were left to prepare these rooms, I wondered why. Mr. Buchanan never allows any gossip. Still, I was curious . . . we all were."

"This isn't a conventional marriage, Lottie, if you're wondering why Caleb and I aren't sharing a room."

Lottie blushed a bright pink. "It might be noticed, but it won't be spoken of. Except maybe by Mrs. Warburton. She's been here so long even Mr. Buchanan lets her rule the place."

"She sounds like a formidable character," Diana smiled.

"Burtie's okay. I like her now! I've learned to jump when she whistles and even Mr. Buchanan pays attention to what she has to say. She came to work here when he was a 'babe-in-arms.' Somehow, it's hard to imagine a 'young' Burtie," she finished.

Diana found it harder to imagine Caleb as a 'babe-in-arms,' although he'd probably looked exactly like Barry did now.

"I must go. I've been talking too much. I hope you won't tell on me," Lottie said, a bit apprehensively.

"You needn't worry about me. I'm more apt to be the one tattled about than the one doing the telling," Diana said.

After Lottie left, Diana found her nightgown and toothbrush. After a quick shower, she climbed into the oversized bed, hoping for quick, dreamless sleep.

It was only as she was drifting on the edge of consciousness that Diana remembered that tonight was her wedding night. Never had she expected to spend it alone.

She was tired, yet she didn't sleep well. The night seemed ages long. Diana wondered why she was so restless. She reasoned that it was probably the strange bed. Somewhere in the middle of the night she decided to take a couple of aspirin, thinking that might help.

As she was returning to bed she heard something. A faint splashing sound.

Curious, Diana stepped silently onto the balcony and walked to the railing to look down below.

There was only a faint sliver of a moon, the shadows cloaked in velvet darkness. It took a minute for her eyes to adjust to the black night.

Below she saw a dark head bobbing above the water. A moment later Caleb hoisted himself out of the pool. She watched as he walked to the diving board and climbed the rungs. It was only as he stood full height, preparing for the dive, that she realized he was nude.

The night was so dark there was actually very little she could see—only an outline—a profile of Adonis. As the figure raised his arms she quickly stepped back. Good grief, what if he'd seen her standing there. He'd think she was spying on his midnight swim. The light-colored gown would be easily discernible even in the dark shadows. She disappeared back into her room.

As her head touched the cool pillow she couldn't help but wonder if he was restless too. Or was a late-night swim a common occurrence? Did he, too, remember he'd acquired a spouse today? That this was their wedding night?

You're crazy, Diana, she scolded herself. She gave her pillow a savage thump. *Forget about being a bride, wedding nights and most of all Caleb Buchanan!*

Chapter Six

It was early the next morning when she heard Barry. Diana listened as he talked to the stuffed animals scattered about his room. He lay in his crib trying out all the new words in his vocabulary, a delightful habit he'd started recently.

I'd better have my shower, she told herself. Although she felt tired after her restless night, Barry would be hungry soon.

Diana dressed in cut-off jeans, a sleeveless sun-top, and sandals. She brushed her hair and pulled it back with a tortoise-shell clip. After applying a touch of lipstick, she went to check on Barry.

He chortled gleefully when he saw her. His funny little way of laughing always caused a quick moment of pain. Gone almost as soon as it happened, something about the way he laughed always reminded her of Deanna.

Diana bathed him and wrapped him in a huge bath sheet, dried him thoroughly, then rubbed baby lotion and talcum all over him, making him smell sweet, baby fresh. His red-brown curls were still damp from his bath, tight springs against his well-shaped head, his dark eyes full of mischief as he squirmed, trying to get away while she dressed him. She dressed him in a one-piece romper, leaving his feet bare. This was one of the best times of the day. No sacrifice was too great—even marriage to Caleb Buchanan!

Unsure of the location of the kitchen, Diana merely followed her instincts and headed in the direction she thought it should be. She met Sterns in the formal dining room, putting freshly polished silver into an antique Dutch *kas*.

"Good morning," he said in his deeply modulated voice. "And to this young man, too."

"This is Barry, Sterns." Diana encouraged Barry to say hello. All he did was bury his head deeper into her shoulder.

"Mrs. Warburton has your breakfast whenever you are ready," Sterns offered, directing her toward the kitchen. As she turned to leave, he added, with a twinkle in his eye, "Her bark is worse than her bite!"

His statement caused Diana a few uneasy qualms as she pushed open the door to the kitchen and prepared herself to meet the redoubtable Mrs. Warburton.

The kitchen decor masterfully blended old and new and was the most down-to-earth room she'd seen since arriving at Twelve Trees. Modern appliances had been built into cypress cabinets and a brick veneer. Small-paned windows, set along arched niches, added a light and airy feeling. Antique copper and pewter pans hung in an organized clutter over a center island, which contained a deep copper sink and wood-planked drain for washing vegetables. A plump little woman who appeared to be about sixty years old stood at the sink. She was mixing something in a bowl.

She glanced up as the door opened. The expression on her lips firmed slightly as she saw who had invaded her domain. "So you're the *new* Mrs. Buchanan," she said, her voice reserved. The statement wasn't a question. "Who is the child?" she added. "Caleb's son?"

"This is Barry." It was all the introduction Diana offered.

Mrs. Warburton sniffed. It clearly meant she'd drawn her own conclusions. She told Diana breakfast would be ready shortly.

One thing soon became apparent to Diana. Mrs. Warburton was a woman of few words. And those were uttered with unnecessary gruffness. Diana sensed that if she was ever to have Mrs. Warburton's approval, it would have to be earned.

While she might be stingy with her greeting, her breakfast was certainly ample. She served country-style sausage, poached eggs, whole wheat biscuits topped with strawberry jam, coffee for Diana and milk for Barry.

They ate the meal on the patio, a terraced sun deck with hanging flowered baskets, its well-tended profusion of sweet smells and flowers alive with honey bees. The deck overlooked an herb and rock garden. Below that a wide expanse of sweeping lawn, green and lush, lay in immaculately clipped splendor. Beyond the lawn, a white latticed gazebo, blue-mirrored lake, and wooded tract were visible. All of this was surrounded by a bridle path also used by joggers. Earlier this morning from her bedroom window, Diana had spied a white-attired figure running along it. She'd suspected Caleb to be the early-A.M. athlete. She'd neither seen him nor heard him mentioned since she'd come down to breakfast.

"No more full," Barry said, holding out his sticky hands in Diana's direction.

She'd just finished wiping his hands when the kitchen door was pushed open and Caleb stepped outside. His eyes were dark, his face with its usual unreadable look.

Dressed in a business suit, he greeted Barry, then turned to Diana. "I need to talk to you before I leave

71

for the office. It's going to add some problems having Irene here. We must be doubly careful. There can't be any way she can connect Barrett with you. I'm convinced she's never heard your name and only knows that he was involved with someone."

His eyes a dark glitter, he continued, "I doubt very much if you'll see her today. She's worn out from traveling. I've arranged for a physical therapist to stay with her.

"Be warned, Diana—stay away from Irene. She's my responsibility and you need not say 'poor Caleb,' either. I'll tolerate no sarcasm from you where Irene's concerned. You are the reason for her unhappiness. They were quarreling about you when the accident happened. I still hold you responsible for her condition as well as Barrett's death."

His eyes were once again fathomless as he looked coldly at Diana. He turned and left, leaving Diana feeling chilled.

It was only when he was reminded of Diana's connection with his brother that the stark coldness came into Caleb's eyes. Of course, Diana thought, there was only one witness to account for what actually *did* happen that night.

Diana couldn't help feeling a bit guilty. She hadn't even met Irene Buchanan and she already disliked the woman. Usually she had more tolerance for human mistakes. Most situations had rights and wrongs on both sides. It was going to be hard being fair-minded.

Diana spent the morning looking over her new surroundings—most of it outdoors, with Barry in tow. After he had finished his nap, Diana decided to give him a swim lesson. The pool would be a temptation. The sooner he learned of the danger, the better.

As she gathered up the towels and lotion, preparing

to leave her bedroom, she caught a glimpse of her figure in the mirrored closet door. The bikini seemed to allow a lot of white skin to show—a good deal more than she remembered! She surveyed her body critically. At least she could say there was nothing wrong with her figure.

The soft bra held the full weight of her breasts, while the bikini bottom was cut high on the sides and seemed to extend the length of her long legs. A sleek, silvery-green geometric design decorated the fabric. She had purchased the suit in a moment of madness two summers before and wondered ever since where she'd found the nerve.

A minute later, Diana descended the circular stairway with Barry in her arms. She stood him on the inlaid tile patio, then deposited the towels and sunscreen on a nearby table. She perched the shaded glasses on her nose.

The beautiful kidney-shaped pool was a shimmering aquamarine blue against gleaming white ceramic tiles. The water felt scrumptious as she tested it with her toe. She walked to the shallow end and sat Barry down on the edge of the pool, enjoying his reaction. A comical expression crossed his face—a puzzled look that was quickly replaced by a crow of delight.

"Bathtub," he said, turning over to slide into the water, tummy first.

Stepping in beside him, Diana held his hand as he took his first steps in the water. She laughed, watching him splash the water, then blink when it went in his eyes.

"Hey, Barry. Open the peepers."

Diana picked him up, carrying him into the deeper section. Her hands under his arms, she pulled him through the water like a small motorboat. He squealed with delight.

Suddenly Diana felt as if they were being watched. Glancing up she was surprised to encounter a pair of dark brown eyes. Caleb was supposed to be at work! She was glad of the covering effect of the water, wishing she'd worn a T-shirt or something—anything— over her brief bikini.

Her dark glasses enabled her to look quite frankly at Caleb's physique. Already tanned to a deep bronze, he wore the briefest of trunks, the scar on his abdomen clearly visible. The hard, flat stomach was marred where the narrowing profusion of hair was interrupted by the wide, jagged imperfection. She remembered seeing it that first night they'd met and wondered where he'd received such a scar.

After a short, shallow dive he was beside her, the dark hair on his chest glistening with beads of water. Guessing quite accurately where she'd been gazing, he said, with tongue-in-cheek humor, "A fencing accident. It almost emasculated me!"

"Too bad," she said, unable to keep the warmth from suffusing her cheeks.

"Too bad it happened, or too bad it missed?" he asked, his voice full of droll wit, his dark-haired arm touching hers. "Or since you aren't sharing my bed yet, perhaps you haven't given it much thought."

"Yet?" she questioned significantly. Again, Diana was glad of the covering effect of the water. She tried, with little success, to calm the butterflies in her stomach caused by the dark warmth she saw in his eyes.

Caleb merely grinned, undisturbed.

"Here, give me Barry." Although watchful, Barry went to him without protesting. Diana was surprised, even a little irritated in fact, though she hated to admit it. It seemed as though he bore no grudges. Caleb's chastisement was forgotten.

Caleb immediately took him under the water. Barry swallowed and choked.

Diana panicked. "He's strangling."

Caleb tersely clipped, "Keep quiet, Diana, or get out of here. I am not going to drown him." His voice brooked no refusal as he added in a low voice, "Your mothering will convince him the water is something to fear."

Caleb took the child beneath the water again. This time Barry handled it better. No choking, although he kept his eyes closed, covered by his hands, once he'd surfaced.

Amazed, Diana watched Caleb take him under the water two more times, each time keeping him under longer. Barry seemed completely at home in the water. Unafraid of Caleb, he was able to hold his breath for several seconds without trying to swallow the pool.

"I'm going to let go of him completely this time," Caleb instructed. "Be ready to catch him."

"You're pushing him too much. He's tired."

"I'm a big boy, Diana. I can make a few decisions if I'm to be his father." He added with emphasis, "And Barry will also get to be a big boy if you will let him."

Diana said nothing, but the black look she gave Caleb spoke volumes.

"Put your hands in front of him," Caleb instructed. "He'll reach out and swim toward you."

Barry did it perfectly. Diana could see him under the water; his eyes were open as he followed her hands. She caught him and pulled him to the surface too quickly. Water went up his nose. He coughed and cried as he tried to gain his breath.

Caleb said curtly, "Let's take him into the shallow end. Maybe if he goes under of his own accord, you won't panic."

Caleb preceded her with Barry in his arms. Diana hesitated, reluctant to leave the protective covering of the water.

But Caleb wasn't interested in her. She watched him pick up a shiny coaster from one of the poolside tables and place it in the water. Barry put his head beneath the surface, his little hand searching, fingers outspread, trying to retrieve the shiny object. Of his own volition, Barry stayed under the water a long time, amazingly unafraid. At his age the learning process was in its fledgling stage and as yet he had developed no fear.

Diana stood by as Caleb repeated the process three or four times. When Caleb turned to give her a triumphant look, she suddenly became aware that his thoughts were no longer on the swimming lesson as he swore under his breath.

Self-consciously she raised her eyes to find his gaze riveted on her bikini—or lack of bikini. Her whole body was on display!

A coppery gleam in his eyes revealed first desire, then anger. He wanted her. It was there in his eyes for her to see. The glaring message of blatant longing was all too familiar to her. His dark brown gaze warmed her skin.

Suddenly an idea began to materialize. What better way of taunting him? Frustrated desire might give her the decisive edge she'd been looking for. It was time Caleb Buchanan was paid back in full for forcing her into this unwilling marriage.

"Is that the *only* suit you have?"

"Really, Caleb! This is the twentieth century. It's called a bikini," she added with irony, her long fingers flicking the water in a saucy gesture, her impertinence daring him.

"That suit is made of nothing but . . ."

"However skimpy, it's made of more than yours was last night." No matter how flippant her attitude, she failed to avoid a certain warmth from coming into her face.

"Restless night? I hope it didn't cause you to lose any *more* sleep!"

"No, but if you'd been the one watching, I'm sure the same wouldn't have been true!" With this saucy answer giving him some food for thought, Diana picked up Barry and went inside, very pleased with herself.

She felt quite clever. She'd definitely won a round. It might take her a while—but she'd have her revenge.

Caleb just barely tolerated her teasing sarcasm. He seemed at odds as to how exactly to deal with it. Diana knew she was treading water in a dangerous zone but she couldn't resist her jibes.

Two whole days passed before Diana met the "other Mrs. Buchanan." Caleb mentioned to her earlier in the day that several friends of long standing would join them for dinner. When Diana murmured she would rather not attend, he *insisted*.

"Be there!" he growled imperiously.

"Haven't you discovered that your wife is a bohemian, Caleb? I'm much more comfortable in jeans and sloppy shirts. Let the 'other' Mrs. Buchanan preside at your table."

"You heard me. Be there, or I'll come drag you there," he clipped, nastily, ". . . by your delectable head of hair."

"I might shock your guests. Cut-off blue jeans at the dinner table?" She smiled sweetly, pleased to incur the sour look she'd expected.

"If you do, you'll wish you hadn't!"

"Don't make idle threats, Caleb."

"They're not idle. Care to try and see?" he challenged her.

She backed out of the threat. He wouldn't be averse to carrying out his promise and she wanted to play for time until she had a better means of reprisal than a childish whim about what she'd wear. Better to bide her time, taunt him, cause that dark look of anger, until one time he'd go too far, and in a moment of unbridled passion, he would declare how much he wanted her in his bed! *Then* she'd have her revenge.

With a secret smile playing across her face, she planned it as she searched through her closet. She would let the tension build over a matter of weeks, months even, giving in a little, now and then, making Caleb think there might be the possibility that she shared his desire. Still, Diana couldn't help feeling some guilt at what she intended to do.

Diana held a dress in front of the mirror, turning from side to side. She wasn't quite able to meet her own eye in the mirror. She lightly shrugged her shoulders. *Caleb Buchanan is a man,* she thought defensively, *more than able to take care of himself.* If she caused him a few sleepless nights of frustration, he probably earned them.

Undoubtedly the path behind him was strewn with more than a few broken hearts. Pity the poor girl who was foolish enough to fall for him. Lots of women thrived on that kind of male chauvinistic treatment, although Diana couldn't imagine anyone being naive enough not to see his underlying ruthlessness and inherent selfishness. She herself would have to be wary or he might manage to turn the tables on her. Diana doubted that his sharp, analytical brain missed much.

She finally decided on an amber dress. It was silk, shot with gold threads, designed in a wraparound style.

She had purchased it for a horrible insurance party and ended up the evening trying to keep it from being "unwrapped" when her choice of a partner had gotten amorous.

She finished dressing, pushing her hair into a silken knot on top of her head. Freshly washed, it had a mind of its own. She'd recombed it several times. Though it still didn't look its best, she was tired of messing with it.

Lottie was staying with Barry. Diana peeked in to check on him, and quickly backed out again as Lottie put her finger to her lips. The tired little boy was just nodding off.

As Diana descended the magnificent staircase, she decided to play the evening by ear. She was nervous about her first encounter with Irene Buchanan and fearful of revealing the wrong thing. Was there any way Irene might guess the connection between Barry and Barrett? And what about Deanna? Had she ever seen a picture? Could she possibly connect the two sisters? There were many unanswered questions, any one of which could cause anxiety, not to mention an impromptu dinner party with a roomful of strangers!

When she entered the library, Diana found everyone there except Irene. Introductions were made.

Abe and Mildred Stafford were neighbors who belonged to Caleb's country club. They were supposed to bring their daughter, Natalie, but she'd gone off in a huff to find greener fields when she'd discovered Caleb was married.

The other guest, Richard Norris, was a widower and a charming older man—florid-faced with big jowls—who was a flirt of the first order. He adored beautiful objects—inanimate and otherwise—and showed his appreciation with sweeping, grandiose statements. "Lovely, lovely, lovely . . ." Richard commented as he walked around Diana. It was as if she were an art object being readied for the auction block. "Exquisite choice, Caleb. Your taste, as always, is impeccable." With a low bow, he kissed Diana's hand.

One of Buchanan's best customers, Richard owned an exceptional collection of jade, which he had started acquiring years before. The collection had increased so much in value that a full-time security guard was essential to make sure it stayed in his family.

Richard Norris and Caleb's grandfather had known each other quite well. "Cameron Buchanan was a law unto himself. If there were ever two alike, it's those two," Richard said as he nodded in Caleb's direction and to the portrait above him. There was a certain arrogance in their carriage, a blatant challenge present in both. The eyes in the picture matched those of the man who stood so casually underneath it. "You'll have your work cut out for you if you tame the likes of him, my dear."

"I'm sure you have Diana shaking in her shoes, Richard," Caleb countered, amusement alive in his voice. Caleb realized full well that Diana was not the least bit afraid of him. "Entertain our guests, *darling*," he encouraged, amusement still close to the surface, "while I go carry Irene in. She hates her wheelchair."

A few minutes later, the two Mrs. Buchanans met.

Irene was petite, her red-outlined mouth like a petulant child's as she smiled up at Caleb. She had lustrous ash blonde hair, exquisite tiny features and a rosebud mouth. Her arms were wound closely around Caleb's neck. She whispered in his ear, undoubtedly her thanks, as he settled her on the sofa. Irene's gaze skimmed over Diana as they were introduced, her ice-blue eyes scathing.

Normally, the library, decorated in mellow woods and soft shades of apricot, gave off a warmth. But suddenly the room felt chilly and cold. For one clear moment, Irene allowed Diana to see her hatred.

Hum, so that's how it is, Diana thought, the venom-filled look amusing her.

"You're Diana. I do hope you don't mind my borrowing your husband," Irene said sweetly, the warmth in her voice never reaching her eyes as they boldly slid over Diana's figure, quickly assessing it, her lips tightening, thinning at what she saw. "I hate to use my wheelchair. It's a constant reminder of many painful memories."

"Any time, any time. I haven't a jealous bone in my body where Caleb's concerned," Diana stated. "Isn't that right, *darling?*" She returned his earlier sarcasm as she raised her eyes to his, letting him see their vivid green depths alive with laughter.

"You're quite a surprise," Irene said. "I can't imagine Caleb married."

"Neither can we!" Mildred Stafford injected into the conversation. "Abe and I mentioned tonight as we drove over how incredible it seemed. Caleb always said he was a 'rolling stone.'"

"It's funny, but I always felt the same way," Diana slipped in. "Our views coincide so much, don't they, Caleb?" His jaw constricted visibly, moving under the taut skin. Diana knew he hated the way she was baiting him, but he was unable to keep her from continuing. "Even the best of us bite the dust sooner or later."

Caleb said nothing, but he gave her a long look as he said, "When you see our son, you'll realize the lateness of the wedding. It was recently I found out about him."

"Son? You have a son?" Irene asked, a slight catch in her voice. She'd spoken so softly it sounded far away, and her hard blue eyes were suddenly bright with tears. "I always wanted a child, too. We quarreled the night

Barrett died. He still wanted to wait." Her words were barely above a whisper. Irene continued talking about that night, but Diana's thoughts were elsewhere.

Irene was acting; Diana was sure of it. It was true that Diana had only Barrett's version of that marriage, but his sincerity had come through. With Irene, the opposite was true. She tried too hard. The result was overkill. This was a polished performance and Diana had to give her an A-plus for the effort.

However, she was relieved to see that Irene acted as if nothing was amiss even when the child's name was mentioned. She was too busy perfecting her actressy execution. But Caleb seemed to be entranced. Even the most difficult of men can have the wool pulled completely over their eyes by a few tears. *Maybe I should resort to a few of my own,* Diana thought, knowing full well it would be extremely unlikely that she would. She never cried, even when the situation warranted it. Irene was making the other dinner guests uncomfortable with her teary performance and Diana was grateful for Abe Stafford's impromptu remark.

"If I had trouble seeing you married, Caleb, the idea of you as a father seems even more farfetched. I can't picture you changing diapers!"

Everyone laughed at the idea, relieving the tension as Sterns came in to announce dinner. He also mentioned that there was a phone call for Mrs. Buchanan.

"It's probably Miss Greene, the physical therapist," Irene explained, her eyes an angry blue. "She's supposed to arrive tomorrow, but she's going to be undependable, I can see." Her lips tight with displeasure, she added, "Probably wants to put me off."

"No, madam," Sterns corrected. "The call is for the other Mrs. Buchanan." He turned to Diana. "A Mr. Brenner."

Diana's gaze went instinctively to Caleb's. She encountered in his face a mask of indifference except in his eyes, which held a dark glitter. Irene measured the look that passed between them, her blue eyes thoughtful.

"I'll take it on the hall phone."

She heard Caleb's clipped reply from the vicinity of her elbow. "Make it short."

But Diana ignored the command and stated brightly, "I'll be right back, everyone." At the library door, she handed her glass to Sterns. "You can serve the dinner, Sterns. I'll hurry."

It was nice to hear a familiar voice say, "Hello."

"Steve, it's great to hear from you."

"You, too, Diana. Just a call to let you know I'll be in town Thursday."

"In Hartford?"

"Have you forgotten we have a branch of Brenner Publishing in Hartford? It's where you originally submitted your illustrations. Remember?"

"Of course, I recall how excited I was. I was on my way to fame and fortune. What brings you to town?"

"The manager of the branch office will be out of circulation for a few months—some badly needed surgery. To make a long story short, I asked Dad if I could fill in. If he suspected an ulterior reason for my wanting to be in Hartford, he never mentioned it. How are things as Mrs. Buchanan?"

"I suppose they could be worse. Caleb is rather bossy, but I happen to be rather spunky, too!"

"Well, if you need me, I'll be near to keep a brotherly eye on you. Seriously, you are okay?"

"Yes. Honest."

"I care, you know." Steve said in a thoughtful tone. "We might not have made it to the altar, but given the chance we could be good friends."

"You're right there. We still can be."

"*If* your husband doesn't object."

"He can't dictate who my friends are," Diana said, unsure whether to believe her own words.

"The Caleb Buchanan I know can accomplish anything he sets his sights on!"

"As I said, I'm spunky," she assured him. "I can give him some food for thought, too! Will you call when you get to town on Thursday?"

"Yes. It will probably be late afternoon."

They said their good-byes, and with a certain reluctance, Diana walked down the hall to the dining room. If she'd been apprehensive about the phone call, she could hardly wait to tell him Steven Brenner was going to be in town for several months. Don't be fainthearted, Diana, she scolded herself. You're just beginning!

Sterns had served the soup as per her instructions. With a curt nod from Caleb she took her place at the opposite end of the table.

"I hope you like cold soup!" he stated.

Eyeing the floating vegetables in a cheese base that Sterns had set in front of her, Diana quipped, "Too bad it isn't vichyssoise!" Diana then murmured her apology to the other guests. They were aware of the tension between herself and Caleb and Irene's thoughtful blue eyes noticed the curt exchange of words before she directed the conversation back to its former subject.

The rest of the meal progressed uneventfully, at least for Diana. She could see why people found Irene charming and sociable. Seated next to Caleb, Irene kept the conversation flowing with practiced ease, her hand lightly touching the sleeve of his dinner jacket. The Staffords and Richard Norris were well entertained —Irene's vitality kept the dinner guests spellbound. But Diana wasn't so lucky. Irene mentioned people and events common to everyone except Diana. She felt like a fifth wheel and knew the slight was deliberate.

When the dessert course was over, Irene asked Richard Norris about the latest acquisition to his jade collection, unaware that she was introducing a topic familiar to Diana.

Beaming, he announced, "I recently added something I thought I'd never own. A Jade of the Sacred Fungus!"

Diana couldn't keep her astonishment from expressing itself in the form of a gasp. Outside of museums, it was an art object almost unheard of in a private collection.

"You know how rare they are?" Richard stated. Amazed, he turned in Diana's direction. "For those who haven't Diana's enlightenment, a JU-1, 'as you desire' rendering in jade is quite unique. It is about the size of a small hammer, intricately carved of the finest transparent jade. It was presented only to noteworthy individuals, usually heads of state, who'd performed some special feat for the emperor during the Opium Wars. To possess one meant your dearest wish was theirs to command. Caleb earned a healthy commission finding it for me."

"I have to admit I was tempted to keep it for myself," Caleb admitted. He turned his eyes on Diana. "How do you know of 'as you desire' jade?"

"How remiss, Caleb," she reproved, clicking her tongue. "My mother managed an antique shop. Remember, darling? Be careful, or you'll give the others the impression we hardly know each other."

"You aren't too informed about your bride, Caleb," Irene inserted, her blue eyes observant, an eyebrow arched.

"We always had 'other things' on our minds. Isn't that right, my love?"

While the others laughed, it was Diana's turn to glare. For once she was grateful to Irene when she suggested they take coffee in her suite. "I have something I want everyone to see. A gift from Caleb." She inserted this tidbit, turning to Diana with a long look as she added, "You don't mind, do you, Diana?"

Diana wasn't sure whether Irene was referring to the gift or the coffee being served in her room. "Of course not," she replied. "I'll ask Sterns to bring it in."

More animated conversation from Irene Buchanan held no appeal for Diana. After she arranged for the coffee service, she played truant. She felt sure Caleb would think of some believable excuse, even though she knew she was being rude. She was also positive her absence would have repercussions as she slipped quietly outside.

The night was balmy with a light wind blowing. It was warm for May. Diana lifted her long hair and allowed the night breeze to touch the nape of her neck, the burnished-gold strands of her hair catching the moonlight with the movement. She pulled the pins from the knot at the top of her head and the heavy weight of it threatened to fall of its own volition.

The round orb of the moon cast the trees and shrubs on the estate grounds into deep shadows. She walked slowly through the damp grass, following the curve of the lake, her strap sandals dangling from her fingertips. A silver-blue streak danced across the water, rippled by a small zephyr of wind. Ahead she could see a small building and below that a pier where paddle boats and a dinghy were tied. She was some distance from Twelve Trees by now but decided the farther she walked, the better.

Moments later, Diana came upon the enclosed summerhouse, an octagon-shaped gazebo. She peered inside the screened building at the cushion-covered benches completely surrounding the outside wall. What a good place for Barry to play!

Diana's thoughts wandered to her work. There was still her contract to be filled. During the past two weeks, with all the earth-shaking events, Diana had sorely neglected her usually faithful adherence to her work schedule. Caleb wouldn't like it, but she intended to finish the illustrations for the children's books. He especially would disagree since it would mean she'd be seeing Steve.

Oh well, she said to herself with a shrug, *he doesn't have to like it.* Remembering she intended to be a thorn in his side, she decided there wasn't any need to worry over that slight problem.

Suddenly her bravado dissipated with the wind as a dark shadow interrupted her thoughts, the stark whiteness of Caleb's dinner shirt bright in the moonlight. What was more surprising was his attitude when he spoke. Although his words were brief, they were more clipped than angry.

"I wondered where you'd wandered off to. Our guests have gone. I suppose you have a good explanation. You don't need to be told that you were rude."

"Irene seemed to be doing such a splendid job of playing hostess, I . . ."

". . . you decided to let her," he finished.

"If you don't know by now, Caleb, I'm not the sugar and honey type. That simpering endless chatter isn't me. Besides, the conversation and people discussed were unknowns as far as I am concerned."

"How do you expect to learn? Twelve Trees is your home, Diana. The Staffords and Richard Norris frequently come to dinner."

"I don't want to learn."

"But you will. This dinner party was sprung on you unawares, but we will have others in the future. I'll introduce you. . . ."

"This marriage was sprung on me unawares! I'm still

having trouble getting used to it. As I said, let Irene play hostess." Diana's eyes were a vivid green in the moonlight, iridescent as cat eyes as she stared at him.

"No, *you*. You're the mistress of Twelve Trees."

"So I am. So I am," Diana murmured.

"Then it's high time you began acting like it," he snapped.

"I promised to make you regret this enforced trip to the altar. You're going to wish you'd let me go," she said with a saccharine-sweet smile.

"We'll see who has more staying power." Then remembering her earlier phone call, he frowned. "What did Steve Brenner want?"

"To speak to me."

"Obviously," he said, his voice full of irony. "You already know my views. Stay away from your ex-lover!"

"Maybe he's just a friend. I'm married to you, but you're dictating who my friends can be wasn't in our vows. I told you that before!" Her eyes again flashed green fire. "Besides, I have a contract to fulfill with Brenner Publishing."

"My wife doesn't need to work."

"I'm not your chattel, Caleb. I need to keep busy. Life would be boring without some challenge. How would you like to spend your days in idleness?"

He didn't answer immediately. Diana knew what was bothering him. Caleb Buchanan hated to give in to anything.

"What about Barry?"

"Barry won't be neglected. He's part of me. But I am an adult, Caleb. I need other diversions to keep my life interesting."

"Like other women's husbands!"

A puzzled frown creased his forehead, his eyes

hooded as he studied her face. Moments passed before he said, his voice abrasive, "It's funny but I can't see you and Barrett. You're totally different from the amiable type he usually went with. Even the way you tilt your chin is like a dare!"

"Maybe he preferred a different type than the one you handpicked for him."

"What's that supposed to mean?"

"I know how Barrett tried to break his engagement and how you insisted he go through with the wedding. He lived to regret your stronger influence."

Diana watched the tight working of Caleb's jaw, his lips thinning. He hated to admit the truth, even to himself. "Maybe he was ready for a woman," she continued. "And not your version in a cold, marble statue."

A moment passed before he shook his head, as if he wanted to rid himself of the thought that his brother had been her lover.

"If I agree to let you continue your painting, I want a promise from you."

"Like what?"

"Like dressing as my wife should."

"I hate to shop."

"I thought all women liked having a new wardrobe. Irene used to adore shopping before the accident."

"I am not Irene." The agitation she was feeling was clearly indicated by the sharp rise and fall of her breasts visible through the low-cut front of her dress.

His gaze seemed to be riveted to the swelling there before returning to her face. "Believe it or not, I do sometimes find her a trial, too!" Caleb said, his white teeth flashing. "Will you agree to my request?"

"On one condition. I only have to be 'the well-draped Mrs. Buchanan' when we have guests at Twelve

Trees. During the rest of the time I can be myself." Then she dared to add, "And Steven Brenner can continue to be my friend!"

There was a long pause as Caleb studied her thoughtfully. Diana hadn't the foggiest idea what he was thinking but somehow she knew there was a silent battle going on.

"That's two conditions," he said.

"I guess I can't count," she agreed, her lips curving in a slight smile.

As she watched him she had an idea. He was acting out of character. Maybe, just maybe, she mused, he thought he'd win her with a little friendly persuasion.

"I'll agree to the first and think about the second. Fair?"

"Awfully fair," she agreed, still puzzled as she tried to figure out his thoughts.

He turned and left.

Diana knew why he left in such a rush—always strong, purposeful and sure of himself, giving in was not normal for Caleb Buchanan.

Diana suddenly began to feel the lateness of the hour, a bit deflated after all the verbal fencing with Caleb. The night air was beginning to chill her. But there was a certain warm glow that remained. Tomorrow she could resume her painting. Plus she felt she'd made a small inroad into figuring out the complex and complicated personality of Caleb Buchanan.

Chapter Seven

As the weeks passed, following Caleb's small concession to allow her to work, life at Twelve Trees settled into a routine. Of Caleb himself, Diana saw very little. True to pattern, he led a disciplined existence. No matter how early she awoke, Diana always found him already involved in his well-ordered life.

Clearly Caleb didn't like the idea of Diana seeing Steve. But, ever watchful, he tolerated it. Steve had visited several times, once even staying for dinner. It had been an uneasy meal, with Steve and Diana laughing, doing most of the talking while Caleb's hooded expression let no nuance escape. Curious about Steve and Diana, Irene scrutinized the scene with a speculative eye—from Steve and Diana's animated laughter to Caleb's guarded look. Because of her friendship with Steve, she was positive Irene would do her best to make mischief and juggle things to her own advantage.

Diana purposely kept quiet regarding certain facts about Steve, facts she was positive Caleb would like to know. For example, Steve had been seriously dating a girl from nearby Avon, a Hartford suburb.

More and more the name of Suzanne Webster came into Steve's conversation whenever he called or dropped by Twelve Trees, which was quite apt to be most any day in the week. Suzanne worked in the same office building where the branch office of Brenner Publishing was located.

"Something between us just clicked." Steve's grin was especially appealing as he added, "Actually it was an elevator that stopped between floors. I had time enough to notice more than Sweet Sue's pretty eyes."

"Lecher!" Diana laughed. But secretly she wished he'd find someone "special," as more and more she found out what a "special" person he was. She wondered what would have happened if it hadn't been for Caleb Buchanan. Then she quickly shrugged it off. No, she and Steve had too much of a brother-sister relationship to have it be different between them.

Caleb had insisted on one condition regarding Steve. Diana was to see him only at Twelve Trees. She'd easily agreed to this provision. Even though Caleb provided her with a car, she rarely used it. She preferred instead to spend her days with Barry, usually at the summer-house, sketching and painting while the child played. Many days she'd even pack a lunch and spend the entire day in the enchanting gazebo. She still found her role as mistress of Twelve Trees overwhelming. The best way to avoid its duties was to stay away from both the house and its master!

The problem with the wardrobe Caleb had insisted she have was easily resolved. Several days after Caleb first mentioned it, stacks and stacks of beautifully packaged boxes arrived and were deposited in her bedroom. Scattering the boxes and tissue over the bed, Diana found they brimmed over with fashion designer clothes, lingerie, and shoes from Hartford's finest store. Surprisingly, everything seemed just right for her coloring and long-limbed figure. Caleb must have a good eye, a fact that didn't surprise her at all. Little escaped his hooded gaze. As for the lingerie, well, she'd never felt anything so fantastic next to her skin—soft silks and shimmering, light-catching satins.

Enclosed was a note. "I thought this might be the easiest way to avoid the dreaded shopping. Caleb."

Too feminine not to admit it had been delightful, she gloried in opening all the boxes. To have all those lovely items without having to step inside a store!

Gradually Diana found Mrs. Warburton was accepting her marriage to her precious Caleb. (She treated him like an indulged son!) When Diana had been there about six weeks, Mrs. Warburton had gruffly told her to call her 'Burtie.'

Diana merely raised an eyebrow slightly before agreeing it would be nice to dispense with the lengthy name. She was aware it was really Barry who had evoked the biggest change in Burtie's attitude. That was easily understood. Hadn't he wrapped himself around her own heart too?

With tongue-in-cheek humor, Diana watched as Barry wormed his way into Burtie's affections, and as each day passed, new things were added to the kitchen, making it better for Barry—an antique highchair, cleaned and polished after years in the storeroom, a whole box of new toys, a cookie jar full of treats. Burtie had even had Sterns fence off a sunny alcove as a place to keep Barry out from under her feet yet under her watchful eye. Several times after this section was divided off, she insisted Diana have some time to herself and sent her exploring on her own, while Burtie cared for the boy.

But it wasn't all sweetness and light where Burtie was concerned. Recently, Diana had arrived downstairs and knew something was amiss when Sterns cleared his throat a couple of times before he hesitantly said, "She's riding her broom today, Mrs. B. You'd be wise to tread lightly." He nodded in the direction of the kitchen. Even without the nod, Diana would have known whom he meant.

The first thing Diana heard as she pushed open the kitchen door, was a curt, "About time!"

As Diana put Barry in his highchair and took a seat at the breakfast nook, she had trouble hiding her amusement as she watched Burtie stomp around the kitchen emphasizing her displeasure with each pot and pan she banged.

"The very least a husband could expect is a warm good-bye when he's out trying to keep the wolf from the door!"

Wolf? Remembering the opulent surroundings of Twelve Trees, Diana felt even more hard pressed to keep a grin from appearing. Burtie reminded her of a small hen with its feathers ruffled as she flounced around. Evidently she thought her "precious" Caleb was overworked.

"Really, Burtie," Diana stated, "wolf at the door seems a bit strong."

The statement was like waving a red flag.

"Maybe, but have you ever taken any wifely interest in what it takes to keep this place and Buchanan's operating in the black? Your husband works day and night. Half a dozen hours of sleep—if that."

She set the plate down in front of Diana with unnecessary force before she added, "He keeps an exhausting schedule. I've never seen him so tired."

Barry observed this unusual Burtie with solemn brown eyes. Clearly even he could tell by the tone of her voice that something was wrong as Burtie gave him a portion of scrambled eggs and toast.

Burtie's voice softened a little as she added, "I don't know what's the matter with him. Something's bothering him. I can tell."

To tell the truth, Diana hadn't seen Caleb. It had

been three days, the last time at dinner, the night Steve dined with them. "Burtie." Diana hesitated, searching for right words. "About our marriage . . . it isn't the usual 'made-in-heaven' variety."

"Name one that is!" Burtie quickly retorted. "If things aren't good between you, fix them. He has too much on his shoulders—the running of Buchanan's, this place, Barrett's wife. Oh, I know you married because of Barry, but you both could end up benefiting from it. Stop mooning over that Mr. Brenner and . . . oh, never mind. It's none of my business anyway," she grumbled as she went out the back door. "I'm going to work in my garden."

Diana hoped the weeds had a quick demise and didn't suffer too much!

"Mad at me?" Barry asked, thinking he was in the wrong.

"No, darlin'," Diana said, setting him in his play area. "Burtie isn't mad at you."

What had all the fuss been about? Evidently Caleb was bothered about something and Burtie wanted to know what. Little missed Burtie's practiced eye. She was well aware that their marriage wasn't the usual kind. As Diana straightened the kitchen, she wondered if it was really possible that Caleb was jealous of Steve Brenner? More than likely it was mere possessiveness.

Diana's thoughts turned to the night Steve had come to dinner. She'd been so engrossed and delighted to be in Steve's company that she'd never noticed Caleb's reaction. She and Steve had enjoyed their usual easy comradery. He had the quick wit that often left Diana searching for an equally witty reply. Diana had exceeded her quota of wine and had been unusually talkative. The opposite had been true of Caleb. He'd talked little and drunk even less. Come to think of it, Caleb and Irene had both seemed merely to observe.

Irene had taken an interest in Steve. "Where did you meet Diana?" she asked, her blue eyes watchful.

"We haven't been friends very long. . . ." Steve managed before he was interrupted.

". . . not just friends," Caleb injected, with terse sharpness. "They were engaged." He might as well have said, "not just friends, but lovers, too."

Over the table Steve and Diana had given each other a long look. Steve had been uncomfortable. Diana knew Steve would have preferred to tell Caleb about their bogus engagement. But Diana had elected to keep Caleb wondering. She'd watched Steve lightly shrug his shoulders, willing to stay quiet if that was what Diana wanted.

"You were aced out by Diana's ploy . . . Barry," Irene said. She watched them, her interest keen. The pale blue eyes deepened to a dark glacial blue as she spoke barely above a whisper. "Maybe you weren't the only one who feels left out, Steve." This time she looked only at Diana.

The mention of the engagement hadn't set well with Caleb either. Although he hadn't commented again, there had been a dark glitter in his eyes.

She heard a slight cough and looked up from her daydreaming to see Sterns standing with a note in his hand. "Come have coffee," the message read. It was signed by Irene.

"A royal summons?" Sterns asked, his kindly face full of sympathy.

"You got it! I wish I'd been elsewhere."

"Would you like me to . . . ?"

"No. I might as well get it over with. Would you please watch Barry for a few minutes?"

With a nod from the sympathetic butler, Diana left the room. The last person she wanted a tête-á-tête with was Irene Buchanan. Caleb wouldn't like it either if he heard about the visit. He'd warned her to stay clear of Irene—one slip and Diana might give the whole charade away. Diana had been inclined to agree. *You'll have to be careful,* she warned herself. Irene Buchanan was as sharp-eyed as Caleb. Diana could easily make a blunder.

Miss Greene, the physical therapist, answered her knock, the nurse's uniform clean and crisply starched. "She'll be grateful for the company. The confinement makes her irritable. Today," Miss Greene said in a low voice, "has been especially harrowing."

The physical therapist hadn't been working for Irene long. Otherwise she might know that Irene's bad temper was a common occurrence.

The suite consisted of two rooms and a bath. An antique grand piano dominated the sitting room, the French Baccarat chandelier mirrored in its highly polished wood. The imported Greek marble fireplace had a beautiful brass-fan firescreen covering its opening. Cream-colored walls were contrasted with the floral-print Aubusson carpet in maroon and leaf-green. The Queen Anne accent chairs were in a cream velour, the loveseat in green.

The nurse left her at the bedroom door and Diana wandered around the bedroom while she waited for Irene to finish a phone conversation.

In a free-standing oval mirror, Diana was able to study Irene unobserved as she lounged against a mountain of lace-edged pillows, half a dozen of them in a variety of sizes artfully arranged at her back. Her nightgown and peignoir were so sheer as to be nonexistent. Was this how she dressed for Caleb's visits? Maybe she thought as a new wife Diana would be jealous if she saw her in this attire? Diana swallowed a feeling of distaste. She was beginning to dislike Irene and her polished elegance. It must have taken years to perfect.

Everything was just right—her appearance, her speech, her mannerisms. Diana composed her face as she heard the end of the phone conversation. She must not let Irene see her annoyance.

"Carolyn, you must come. Twelve Trees is so beautiful. I want to share it with my oldest friends." Irene laughed, her voice a lilting musical chime. A long polished nail tapped a rhythmic pattern on the shimmering bedspread. "Do plan to stay the day, darling, if you can't manage an overnight visit." There was another pause, then the laugh again, before she added, "Fabulous. See you then."

As soon as she replaced the phone Irene gestured to the chair beside the bed, her cold blue eyes on Diana as she rang for coffee. "Sorry to keep you waiting. The phone has become my life since the accident. It seems my only enjoyment is to organize a few little dinner parties or visits with friends." The words were meant to invoke sympathy as they waited for the nurse to appear. Diana nodded as she listened to Irene's condescending order to the nurse. "Serve us coffee, Greene."

Turning to Diana, she said, "Now, tell me about your new wardrobe."

"You know about that?"

"Lottie," Irene confessed. "She was bubbling over about your new clothes. I happened to notice it. Don't be mad at her gossiping."

Diana doubted if Irene happened to notice anything.

"It isn't likely anyone could be upset with Lottie for long."

Irene nodded with a bored look. A trivial matter, her eyes said. Diana knew Lottie didn't feel so benevolent toward Irene. She had already expressed her dislike of Irene's orders.

"I assume those aren't your new things?" Her eyes

went carefully over Diana's clothing. The cotton shirt and shorts, while neat and clean, were definitely not new.

"No. It will take some getting used to—a designer wardrobe. Not my usual thing," Diana added.

"And I'd love it," Irene inserted. "Shopping can turn the most dismal day into sunshine. At least it did . . . before that!" She pointed to the wheelchair, her blue eyes bright with unshed tears or . . . hatred? Her satin-smooth hair seemed to shake with repressed anger. "I've always dreamed of coming here as mistress of Twelve Trees . . . wearing beautiful clothes. But Barrett wouldn't live here. He insisted we have our own place. I couldn't budge him . . . nor could Caleb."

"Caleb wanted you to live at Twelve Trees?"

"Oh yes, he thought I'd make the perfect . . . addition." Then, as though she suddenly remembered something she'd wanted to ask, she said, "Tell me, where did you meet Caleb?"

Here it comes, Diana thought. I knew there had to be a reason for the invitation. "I'd prefer not to talk about my *lurid* past!" Diana almost laughed. Her choice of words had Irene's attention.

"Lurid?" Irene raised a finely plucked brow.

"There must have been some sensationalism. We do have . . . our son!" Diana avoided repetition of Barry's name, afraid Irene would guess the connection between his name and Barrett's.

"Is he the reason you married?" Irene paused, her blue eyes cold as a glacial lake. "It is one snare I never thought about using. Caleb always said he'd never marry."

It was Diana's turn to raise an eyebrow. "Caleb?" Diana questioned.

"It's a little-known secret. Barrett always was second choice."

Shock waves shot through Diana, making her careless.

"Then why wouldn't you divorce Barrett?"

"You knew he wanted a divorce? You speak as though you might have known him?" Irene's eyes were watchful as they looked at Diana.

Cold fear shook Diana's usual poise. What was she saying? Was it too late to retrace her steps without giving herself away even farther? She trembled. She hated to think what Caleb would do if Irene guessed the connection between his brother and Barry.

"Caleb must have mentioned that . . . your husband wanted . . . out. It just seems such a waste. Married to one brother, in love with another."

"The feelings weren't only on my side. They were reciprocated, too. But Caleb was marriage shy . . . incidents that happened before we met. I wouldn't want you to say anything to him. He probably wants to forget what we meant to each other. We were waiting for a suitable time, then he found out about your child." She paused, looking at Diana's white face.

"I'm sorry, I can see I've upset you." While Irene's eyes were glacial deep, the corner of her mouth turned up as though she was especially pleased about something. Diana was too shaken about her near miss to care what it might be. She had to get out of Irene's suite.

But like it or not, Diana had to sit and listen to more trivial conversation. At least this time it seemed to be on safer subjects—the weather, the neighbors, and the vast hordes of friends that would soon descend on Twelve Trees if Irene was to be believed. After a hasty cup of coffee, Diana mentioned she had to leave.

"You're bored," Irene said.

For one insane second Diana was tempted to say

"yes." But Irene wouldn't find her "yes" answer at all humorous. "Of course not," she assured her.

"Please do come again tomorrow." Irene reached across the space between them and took the cup and saucer from Diana with a hard jerk.

The sudden movement took Diana by surprise. The dishes seemed to fly out of her hand, the dregs from the cup wetting the bedspread and the dishes landing in a broken heap on the hardwood floor.

"Oh! How clumsy!" Irene quickly injected, a little too quickly unless she'd been expecting something to happen!

She acted as though it was Diana's fault, when in reality the opposite was true. It had been deliberate, and they both knew it. Diana could see the triumphant gleam in Irene's eyes. But the success of her trouble-making worked even better than Irene had dreamed.

Then something happened that made them forget about the broken china.

Irene moved her foot! Beneath the satin-smooth bedspread, in the vicinity of where her legs were, there had been movement!

It happened so fast, Diana wasn't sure. "You moved your foot."

"Moved my foot? What are you talking about?" The blue eyes were diamond bright. They glared at Diana in deep hatred. "Would I be here in this bed, if I could walk?"

"I said you moved your foot—not that you can walk. You did move it, didn't you?"

Irene picked up the bell beside the bed and shook it vigorously. Moments later, Miss Greene appeared. "Mrs. Buchanan broke her cup and saucer. You'll have to clean it up as soon as you've shown her out."

Diana had been standing stone-still, wondering

about the implications behind the movement of her foot. What did it mean? Was it possible the feeling was returning to Irene's legs? She finally found her voice. "I can find my own way out. Take care of your invalid!" Without a backward glance she went out the door.

Diana heard Irene say before she was out of earshot, "Get me my tablets before you do anything. My head is killing me." She sounded upset.

Once in the hall, Diana had to squelch the desire to run. What a nasty person! Barrett's description of his wife had been too nice!

Diana felt the need for fresh air. She stopped into the kitchen only long enough to fix a lunch for herself and Barry. The gazebo would provide the needed clean air after the visit with Irene.

The sun had yet to reach its zenith, but already it was hot. Diana hadn't been herself of late. She'd always been able to get rid of the doldrums by painting. But, it wasn't working. Lately she'd thrown away more sketches than she'd kept. Today would be different.

Maybe the new illustrations would help. The setting around the gazebo was perfect. The book was full of boats, lakes, and billowy clouds. In watercolors, too. A favorite expression of her art.

They ate lunch, after which Barry nodded off.

An hour later Lottie arrived all in a huff.

Diana laughed. "Everyone is a little insane. I haven't been myself, then Burtie, and now you arrive feeling grumpy."

"Not me. It's her! She's a witch. Nothing can please her," Lottie emphasized, her dark curls dancing. She spoke in an agitated hush so she wouldn't wake Barry.

"Who?" Diana asked, already sure she knew.

Lottie's cheeks were fused with red. "I went to stay with Mrs. Buchanan while Miss Greene ran an errand. Do you know what terrible deed I did? I opened the door of her suite without knocking! An absolute no-no!"

Diana smiled, amused. "A hanging offense."

Lottie was quiet a moment, her eyes thoughtful before she added, "You want to know why I think she was so upset? She was afraid. A minute earlier and I'd have caught her walking!"

"Walking!" She had Diana's full attention now. This was an interesting speculation after the incident this morning. No wonder Irene had been visibly shaken. She'd nearly given herself away. Diana decided to keep the news to herself. Lottie might forget and blurt it out. An element of surprise wouldn't hurt if it was true. What would Caleb think if his precious Irene had been playing games and had been able to walk all along? "Go on, Lottie. Tell me more."

"Miss Greene said she'd left her asleep on the bed. She warned me to be quiet. But when I arrived Mrs. Buchanan was in the next room, on the chaise lounge, looking out the window! When she saw me she started to yell." Lottie shrugged her shoulders. "Maybe, I'm wrong. Perhaps I misunderstood Miss Greene. I don't like Irene Buchanan and she knows it. I feel sorry for poor Mr. Buchanan. He can't get rid of her. She sticks like glue."

Diana smiled at her defense of Caleb. He seemed well-championed. First Burtie, now Lottie was determined to help his cause. It amused Diana.

"Why pretend not to walk? It would be boring to be confined if it wasn't necessary. Caleb gives her plenty of his time so she couldn't be doing it as a way to get his attention. She has the run of the place—donating to charities, inviting all and sundry to visit. And he'd end her extravagances if he wanted her to leave. You must be mistaken, Lottie."

"You're probably right," Lottie agreed. Her lips

relaxed and she lost some of her pouty expression. "Still why was it necessary to scream at me?"

Diana's own thoughts were racing at breakneck speed and weren't so benevolent as she voiced to Lottie. She intended to get to the bottom of the mystery. Was Irene Buchanan making fools of all of them? "Maybe she's having a bad day. I saw her earlier and when I left she seemed upset. But I heard her ask for her tablets as I went out the door."

"In a little teary voice, I bet," Lottie inserted. "She's always crying about something and Mr. Buchanan is a real pushover when she turns on the water! You ought to try it," Lottie added. "He's really a marshmallow when it comes to tears."

Diana laughed with genuine mirth. "Caleb a marshmallow!" Somehow it didn't fit. Lottie laughed, too. It was a ridiculous description!

"Maybe a buttercup would fit better." They laughed even harder, waking Barry. He whimpered a second, rubbing sleep from his eyes. When he saw who was there, he raised his arms to his "Ottie."

Lottie took a few minutes to play with him before she decided she'd better leave. She'd played truant long enough.

After she'd gone, Diana thought about what had been said about Irene's walking. If it were true, she'd made a near fatal mistake almost letting Lottie catch her walking. The wheelchair a room's length away was pretty incriminating evidence.

Combined with Irene's error this morning, that made two mistakes in one day!

If it were true, Diana was curious about Irene's reasons for doing it. And she intended to find out. She could play a waiting game, too. The opportunity would arrive sooner or later. Until then she would bide her time.

Chapter Eight

Diana found Burtie somewhat more amiable after her burst of bad temper. Evidently, she felt a bit chagrined about her anger over Steve Brenner's visit. Over the next several days the house seemed more complacent, at least while Burtie wasn't on the warpath. Normally, Burtie was very closemouthed, but lately she'd been unusually friendly. Diana had learned a good deal from her, mostly about Caleb's childhood. Diana doubted he'd have liked it if he'd known. Burtie made him seem almost human.

"Thank you for breakfast," Diana said one morning. "It was delicious, as always. Barry likes your fare, too," Diana said, wiping Barry's hands and face before lifting him down from his highchair. "Yum, Barry?"

"Yum," Barry echoed, his grin sporting a brand new tooth. Diana settled him in his play area.

"You have your talents, too," Burtie stated, her voice gruff.

Diana's eyes widened in surprise as she turned to stare at the woman. Praise from Mrs. Warburton was praise indeed. "Talents?" Diana asked, curious.

"You take good care of Barry. You're quite a good mother."

"I never thought of motherhood as a talent."

"Never having had any of my own, I wouldn't know.

But I have seen the devastating effects of a mother's desertion on a young boy."

"You mean Caleb's mother?"

"The same. He was just seventeen. She'd always been pretty good with the boys until then."

Diana couldn't help thinking that Burtie hated to admit Caleb's mother had ever been a good parent. Even after all these years, fourteen to be exact, it was still a touchy subject. Burtie was kneading a batch of bread dough and her small, compact figure shook as she pounded the mixture.

"There was an artist," Burtie continued. "He was supposed to be a good one, although I'm unfamiliar with such things. He came to paint Mrs. Buchanan's picture. In the end they ran off together. After that Caleb's father let the business fall apart. Took to drink, he did. Caleb blamed his mother. There were signs that the older Mr. Buchanan was already having a problem with alcohol before . . ."

". . . before his mother ran away," Diana injected into the conversation. "But Caleb wouldn't see that. Everything is either black or white with Caleb. No shades of gray."

"He was just seventeen, remember!" Burtie said, defensively. "If that wasn't enough, his father died under mysterious circumstances. An avid sailor, he took a sailboat out in questionable weather. Caleb always wondered if he'd done it deliberately and blamed himself for allowing him to go. Perhaps he would have been more tolerant if he'd been older and the timing had been different. Caleb was just beginning to understand, to mellow a bit about his mother's leaving and his father's death. But something happened to change all that. The news got out about the precarious state of affairs at Buchanan's. Caleb was twenty-three at the time and engaged to be married. His future bride dumped him for someone else—a well-heeled someone else! How could the little two-timer ever guess what would happen?" Real mirth came into her eyes as Burtie added, "It didn't take her newly acquired husband long to go bankrupt. They'd only been married a short while. At the same time, Caleb managed to put Buchanan's back at the top!"

The pride was evident in her voice. "I witnessed the joyous reunion. It was supposed to reunite them. The ink from her divorce papers barely dry, the ex-Mrs. Adair thought Caleb would welcome her back with open arms. He never raised his voice, just cut her down to size with cold words. Velvet steel, I call it."

Diana remembered the chilly reception she'd received the first time she had met him. A shiver traveled down her spine with the memory of that dark, stormy night. Yes, velvet steel was exactly right.

"Think about it," she heard Burtie say. "He seems hard and cold, but underneath . . . underneath he'd be putty in the hands of the right woman."

"Don't fantasize about our marriage, Burtie. I know you care about Caleb. I've seen the affection between you. But don't . . ." Diana said, trying to pick her words carefully, not wanting to hurt the older woman. But she did need to make Burtie understand. "Don't . . ."

"Are you sure nothing's there?" Burtie interrupted. "What you both need is a good knock on the head. You're two healthy young animals. You might find some solace in each other's arms if you would just look!

"Why do you suppose he does all that crazy exercising—aeorbic or whatever he calls it?" Burtie asked. "He says it gives him more energy. I say it is also an outlet, it lets him forget there are things money can't buy—a loving wife and family, someone to tell him they care." Then as an afterthought Burtie added, "Have you ever seen him work out in the gym?"

When Diana shook her head, Burtie continued, "No? I'll watch Barry. Walk down to the gym and peek in the window. You might be amazed. Go on with you. Barry will be just fine."

Diana could see he was safely contained in his play area, already absorbed in building some creation out of attachable plastic pieces. A favorite pastime. So she did as Burtie suggested and left him to play.

Once outside, she strolled along the grounds, realizing only as the gymnasium came into view that she'd subconsciously followed Burtie's instructions. At least she hadn't consciously thought about where she was going—not until the building was in front of her.

Through the open window Diana could hear a rhythmic thump. Cautiously, she edged closer until she could peek into the room.

The room was painted with a geometric design. A broad stripe of blue and green was woven against a stark white background. A large portion of the floor was covered by thick white exercise pads, while skylights brought the outdoors inside. Plants and greenery were in every corner and mirrors lined the walls. The room was outfitted with the finest, most up-to-date equipment available—rings, parallel bars, horse, and two trampolines. Everything was made from shiny chrome and steel.

Diana watched as Caleb's body, agile as a cat's, formed an arc and landed easily on the mat. He was comfortably dressed for gymnastics in a knit singlet and form-fitting gym pants. White tape circled his wrists.

As always, Diana couldn't help but admire his superb physique. Half of her wanted to become part of him; the other half said to run, warning her against a melting softness inside that manifested itself whenever she happened to see him.

Was her body responding to its need for a mate? Whatever it was, she'd be wise to push the newly awakened cravings out of her mind. She had need of a warning, the way her traitorous thoughts had been behaving. Any physical relationship with Caleb Buchanan was absolutely impossible!

Admiring his performance, she continued to observe his prowess on the horse, followed by the parallel bars and lastly the rings. He sprang lightly, catching the rings, swinging into a practice drill. His body was graceful, arching and swaying, holding a handstand, denying the strength needed to do the exercise. He made it seem almost easy!

There wasn't any question about it—he was good. The trophies by the entry had undoubtedly been earned by Caleb. Had he been an Olympic contender? Diana wasn't any judge of the requirements needed to compete, but he certainly appeared to be good enough.

She watched as he brought the rings to a sudden, abrupt stop, holding his arms straight out parallel with the floor in an Iron Cross. He held the position as a minute passed . . . then another. His arms began to tremble with exertion, sweat breaking out on his forehead. Finally, exhausted, he dropped to the floor, breathing deeply, sucking in air. He bent his body, his head between his knees, his hands almost touching the floor, filling his lungs with the much needed oxygen.

He straightened, reaching for a towel that hung conveniently nearby. With it he wiped the beads of sweat from his brow, then dropped the towel around his neck and headed for the showers.

Diana ducked out of sight, afraid Caleb might glance up at the window and see her spying. A few seconds later she was back on the path, headed in the opposite direction from the gym.

No matter how much she had tried to deny its existence, the woman inside responded to what she had just seen—the first awakenings of desire for the man she called husband.

What would he be like as a lover? To be loved, and made love to by Caleb Buchanan? Have those strong arms hold her close, have him kiss her senseless with need, his hands slowly undress her. . . .

Even as she hurried away Diana tried to convince herself with little success that she was running away so Caleb wouldn't catch her spying. But deep inside she knew the real reason!

It was only three days later that Diana had the opportunity to find some answers to her questioning thoughts.

It had been a long walk back to the house from the stables. Diana sat down in the grassy area below the patio and took off her shoes. Wiggling her toes in the newly clipped grass, she watched amused as Barry mimicked her actions.

"Tickles, hmm, Barry?"

The sensation was a new one to him. And from the look on his face, one he wasn't sure he liked.

They'd been on a picture-taking spree, with Barry as the subject and Diana as the official photographer. She couldn't wait to see the results. She was a very enthusiastic amateur, clicking away with the new Nikon while Barry cooperated by being delightful. A month-old colt had made a charming subject, too. They'd made the trip to the stable to see the new addition.

Content and at peace with her world, Diana rested for a few minutes, lying back watching Barry. Happy and satisfied, she thought that her life at Twelve Trees wasn't as bad as she'd once anticipated.

Caleb, too, seemed pleased about their arrangement, only occasionally pausing long enough in his busy schedule to give her some marked attention regarding their mutual parenting of Barry.

She glanced at the Nikon camera, which lay beside her on the grass. Caleb had given it to her. He'd used it to mollify a relatively minor disagreement, one she'd already forgotten about.

Caleb had seemed almost boyish when he'd presented it, embarrassed even. His voice had been brusque, as though he couldn't have her guessing what had prompted him to purchase it, what his real feelings might have been. He'd hurried away quickly.

Could Burtie be right? Would Caleb be putty in the hands of a woman he really cared about? Somehow, the description wasn't as far fetched as it once would have been. Too many times she'd seen him with Barry to doubt his genuine affection where Barrett's son was concerned, and with Burtie, too. The love between them was real. Burtie had her own little house. He'd even offered her rooms at Twelve Trees but she'd refused, preferring her own place and garden. So he had purchased the house and had given it to her.

Was the reason behind that hardened exterior to deter anyone from getting too close? The velvet steel— was it to hide what he considered a weakness? Maybe his first love meant something to him still? Once bit, twice shy? For some elusive reason, that thought bothered Diana. She didn't want Caleb carrying around a torch for some long-ago love. She wanted his undivided attention. She'd only seen one piece of evidence of any susceptibility—the fact that he was such an easy mark over a woman's tears. Since she never cried, Diana wasn't likely to use that as a weapon. She'd leave the waterworks for Irene.

Diana knew she'd need to keep a tight grip on her own feelings. She didn't want to be the least bit vulnerable where Caleb was concerned. She didn't want to find herself thinking of him too often. She swallowed down a feeling of panic. There never could be any relationship between herself and Caleb Buchanan!

It was Barry's tugging on her arm that brought her out of her reverie. It seemed Barry wasn't content to have her lie there watching the clouds. He wanted to be swung around like a monkey. Taking him by the arms, she complied.

Diana whirled him around and around on the green lawn in a slightly drunken, ever widening circle. Her toffee-colored hair glinted in the bright sun, her long hair floated and swirled about her head. With a flash of slender golden-brown legs, the two of them tilted, overbalanced, and accompanied by a chortle of laughter from Barry, collapsed in the newly mowed grass.

She lay there catching her breath, watching Barry, amused as he tried to stand. Evidently, the landscape was still spinning, since his walk was a bit more wobbly than usual. His reddish-brown curls caught the bright sunlight as he toppled beside her again. "Dee-dee loves you, funny-face," she said, pulling on one of his tightly sprung curls.

Barry demonstrated his love with a slightly slobbery kiss and dimpled arms thrown around her neck in a tight squeeze. He pointed to a spot near her chin. "Bug?" he asked.

It was a word he knew. On several occasions Diana had pointed out little "creepy crawlers." Diana let out a squeal and brushed her hand where he had pointed. Her hand came away with a blade of grass.

112

"You?" Diana gasped with relief and laughter. "You little scamp, you! Scare me to pieces, will you?"

Gathering up a handful of newly clipped "bugs," she piled them playfully on top of Barry's head, repaying him in kind. It wasn't long before both of them were covered with grass clippings—Diana's white shorts and shirt and Barry's play clothes speckled with green blades. The grass adhered to them as they tumbled around like puppies.

As they played, Diana was unaware that they were being observed. From the terrace two pairs of eyes solemnly watched their frolicking, neither Caleb nor Burtie showing any amusement as the laughter drifted into their hearing range.

"She is beautiful, your wife," Burtie stated. "And Barry is a handsome boy. You wish he was your son?"

The dark eyes opened slightly, amusement curving his mobile mouth as Caleb smiled at his observant little housekeeper. Little missed her notice. A look of affection passed between them. They'd always had a very special relationship, evident to everyone even mildly acquainted with the two of them.

"He is a good-looking boy, isn't he? Looks just like me," Caleb said with a conceited grin.

"But he isn't yours. He's Barrett's."

Burtie observed a fleeting, pain-filled expression on Caleb's face. It lasted only a moment before he answered, his features once again in control, "Yes. I wish he were mine."

"Your wife, you wish she were yours, too?" This time Caleb raised an expressive eyebrow, a slight smile that showed he understood as she continued, "Your bedrooms are half a house away from each other. The hall carpet doesn't appear to be worn!"

Burtie heard a soft chuckle as she continued, "Your wife is heart-whole. I'm sure she got over Barrett a long time ago. And she has a nice full bosom." With a rueful smile, she added, glancing at her own ample bust, "My husband always used to say it was the softest spot on earth."

Caleb's mouth curved even more. His eyes riveted on the figure below, the tautness of her blouse. "It's a pillow I've thought some about."

Suddenly their musing was interrupted by a scream of pain. It came from below. Barry!

"What is it, Barry?" Diana asked, alarmed. "Tell Dee-dee where it hurts?"

Frantically she searched for the source of pain. Barry rarely cried and she knew he was hurting by his reaction.

By this time Caleb had reached them. Squatting, he quickly pulled Barry's shirt off, saying, "It must be an insect bite. A bee most likely." Then to Barry he said, "Son, show Dad where it hurts."

Sobbing, Barry wrapped his arms around Caleb's neck, certain in his little mind that "Dad" could make it better.

Distraught, Diana, too, turned to Caleb. "What is it?"

It was Barry who told them.

"Shoe hurt." He held up one small bare foot for their inspection.

A second later, Diana and Caleb saw the stinger embedded in the sole of his foot. Caleb picked Barry up and with a long stride carried him swiftly across the lawn. Diana found that even with her own long legs she had trouble keeping pace with Caleb's lengthy steps.

Caleb and Burtie dealt expertly with the bite. Caleb set Barry on the kitchen table, while Burtie already had a pair of tweezers in hand. They disposed quickly of the stinger.

Diana watched as Burtie squeezed some gellike substance from a cactus plant she had in the kitchen window. Cutting through its fanlike leaf she used the gel from the wounded plant on the angry red swelling. By this time Barry's crying had subsided into quiet hiccups, his nose running as he watched Burtie's ministrations.

Diana wiped Barry's nose with a tissue, holding him close while Burtie reassured her the aloe vera gel should take the swelling down.

The last soothing touch was a popsicle for Barry. "Root beer," Burtie said. "It matches his eyes, just like his Dad's!" As she said this, she glanced first at Caleb with a knowing look, followed by an observing one in Diana's direction. "Take him upstairs, it's his nap time. A nap probably wouldn't hurt your wife, either, Caleb." With another meaningful glance in his direction, Burtie added, "She looks anxious."

With a secret smile on her face, Burtie returned to the preparations for the evening dinner as Caleb directed his family upstairs, Barry in his arms, his hand under Diana's elbow guiding her.

More shaken than she'd like to admit, Diana allowed Caleb to take complete charge. A few minutes later, after Barry had finished his treat, Caleb washed his face and hands. Barry then, without much coaxing, nodded off while Caleb and Diana looked on.

It wasn't until Barry fell into a restful sleep that Caleb noticed Diana's white face and the strained look around her eyes.

"You look as if you're ready to cry."

"I never cry."

"Are you sure the flood waters aren't just below the surface?" Caleb teased. He reached across the space between them and drew Diana against his shirtfront,

115

wrapping his arms protectively around her as they gazed down at the sleeping child. "Barry's all right, babe. Look at his foot. The swelling has already subsided."

Enjoying the protective circle of his arms, Diana allowed her head to rest against his chin. Her voice was a husky whisper, full of emotion. "In those few seconds before we found out what was wrong—" She swallowed hard a couple of times. "He's my responsibility. If anything happened to him . . ." Her words trailed off as she shuddered against him.

"He's my responsibility, too, Diana." Caleb's voice was full of quiet authority as he added, "From now on, you're going to share it with me."

He swung her into his arms, his hands warm on her bare legs as he carried her to her room. He ignored her protest of: "I'm too heavy!"

"A nice armful."

His voice was light, teasing as he pulled back the bedspread and laid her gently on the cool sheets before disappearing into the adjoining bath. Moments later he returned with a wet cloth for her face. "If you didn't fight so hard to hold back the tears, you might feel better for them." His voice was full of gentle concern. "You do have a husband now to help you over the rough spots."

"I always did wait until a crisis was over to fall apart."

"So fall apart. I'm here." He lay down beside her on the bed, pulling her face against his warm throat.

Suddenly it seemed the right thing to do, to share the worry and responsibility of raising Barry. A few tears surfaced in spite of her valiant efforts. She brushed them away with an impatient hand. At the same time, she heard a soft "shh" sound from Caleb's throat as he pulled her closer still. He pushed the silky curtain of hair aside, framing her face with his hand, staring at her with unreadable eyes.

How long the comforting continued Diana wasn't sure. Or when it changed. Physical desire flared like a bright flame between them.

A searing trail of kisses sent a surge of feeling through her body. She gasped at the unexpected feeling as his lips first took possession of her mouth, then moved to the tender hollow of her throat before traveling to the pulse point visible near her ear. His mouth created a throbbing confusion, a sweet longing that achingly clamored for his complete possession.

Another searching, hungry kiss tinged with possessiveness made her heart lurch in nervous excitement and seemed to go on forever in its undeniably passionate exploring, probing. It wasn't until her blouse was opened and cool air touched her skin that Diana realized Caleb's hands had been as searching as his kisses. But it didn't frighten her.

He had the most deliciously slow hands. Every movement was designed to make her tremble with awareness. A crazy, wild singing was in her ears. Her body felt as if it had been quiescent for years and was slowly coming to life under his touch. He brushed her navel with his long fingers, then his lips. The sensation seemed to create a curling sensation that went all the way to her toes, then spread outward and upward through her loins like liquid fire.

His eyes held a dark lambent flame as they gazed at the half-revealed skin of her shoulders and breasts through the lacy bra. His stroking fingers continued their languid stroll following the curve of her body and came to rest near her wildly clamoring heart.

Caleb's hand trembled visibly, fumbling at the front closure of her bra. She watched through covert lashes as the dark irises of his eyes turned even darker, his hand cupping, his thumb brushing across a rosy tip. A small moan of pleasure escaped from between her kiss-swollen lips. Of its own volition her body arched closer as his thumb continued its lazy circle. Then his dark head moved lower, replacing his hand, kissing the soft valley and curves, using his tongue to assuage the aching bud.

Her head moved back and forth on the pillow. The sensations he was creating were almost too overwhelming. It was like being caught by a wave of feeling, helplessly tossed back and forth.

Moving closer, and guided by instinct, Diana encircled his waist. With shaky hands she unbuttoned his shirt, touching him, enjoying the feeling of his firm, taut skin. She slipped her hand inside, loving the feel of the wiry chest hair against her palm, brushing the dark nipples bedded there. She heard his quickened breath, which he expelled in a near-groan. It gave her a heady feeling of power.

He lifted his head, a perplexing frown on his face. "You're trembling."

"It's nothing," she whispered, her voice husky.

"Are you afraid? You seem so shy, almost virginal!" A look of anger replaced the frown. "Ridiculous, huh!"

Fear shot through Diana as she realized how close to the truth he actually was. It was as effective as a cold shower would have been. She pushed herself to a sitting position and with trembling fingers, clumsily pulled her blouse over her sensitized breasts.

"What's wrong?" said a deep voice. "I want to stay."

"No!"

"You wanted me a moment ago. There are ways a man can tell. Why change your mind?" Standing up beside the bed, his eyes never left her face as Caleb tucked his shirt back inside his pants. Diana watched him, her gaze veiled by long lashes, unable to meet his eye. Both of them knew who had pulled the shirt loose.

"You are only postponing the inevitable," he said fatefully. "Whatever it was that made you change your mind," he paused, tossing her a warning, "It's only a matter of time!" The sound of a well-slammed door echoed across the room.

After he'd gone, Diana studied her image in the freestanding mirror beside the bed. Wide-eyed, she stared at her love-softened face. There was something there she'd never seen before—a warmth, a certain radiance in her eyes.

Frightened by her own reactions, Diana knew it would be necessary to keep a close tab on her emotions and guard against being alone with Caleb. He must never know she wasn't Barry's mother!

Chapter Nine

Diana finished packing her bag while Caleb brought the Mercedes around to the front. It had been several days since he'd suggested they spend a long weekend at Woodledge. She had misgivings about returning. It wasn't because of Deanna and Barrett and the fact that Woodledge was the setting of their ill-starred love affair, but mainly because she'd had her first encounter with Caleb Buchanan there. The name of the place sent her into a panic.

Diana hadn't been herself lately. Easily irritated, she blamed her bad temper on the humid weather. Energy-sapping mugginess would make anyone blow her cool, she rationalized. But she recognized that this wasn't the whole of it. Caleb constituted a goodly portion of her irritability. She couldn't restrain the tartness on her tongue whenever she was near him. It had been days since they'd spoken a civil word to each other. She knew the bulk of blame belonged on her shoulders.

Caleb had withstood several weeks of this on-again, off-again bad temper before he retaliated in kind. One evening, after Diana's particularly snappish reply to a question from Irene, he exploded.

"Would you excuse us, please?" he said, addressing Irene. "I need to speak to my wife!"

There wasn't even time to let Irene enjoy her triumphant little smile. Moments later, Diana was literally shoved into the sitting room.

"All right, out with it. What in the hell is the matter with you lately?" Caleb snapped. "You are turning into a shrew. Nobody can say a single word to you without your coming unglued. Would you mind enlightening me as to the cause?"

Diana shrugged her shoulders. She wished she could blame it on the weather or Irene. Twenty days with the weather near the hundred-degree mark didn't help, nor did Irene's sly little innuendos, but they really didn't bother Diana all that much. Truthfully, they amused her more than anything else.

No, it wasn't the weather or Irene. It was Caleb. How much longer would it be before he declared himself? He kept his feelings locked behind a mask of indifference. She couldn't begin to guess what he was thinking.

His dark eyes were hard as he asked again, "Well, are you going to tell me?" Then he added, his voice even more vehement, "It's not just toward me, either. Irene, Lottie, even Barry hasn't escaped."

Unable to meet his eyes, Diana merely shrugged her shoulders again.

Caleb stepped toward her, his hands outstretched as though he wanted to shake her. Instead he stopped midstride. He slammed his fist into the open palm of his hand, releasing the energy.

"Well, whatever the reason, this is the end of it. I've had all I want of your bad temper." This last he added with a dangerous tone to his voice.

"It can't just be me," Diana said, her head beginning to ache with the tension.

"Most of it is. I'll make the arrangements—ask the Staffords, maybe the Martins. We'll spend a few days at

Woodledge. It'll do you good to have a break. You can leave Barry with Lottie. She had a houseful of brothers and sisters. She'll take good care of him."

"I've only been away from him for one night."

"All the more reason."

Perhaps he is right, Diana thought, finding herself agreeing. She was turning into a "nagging scold." It would be a welcome change to be away from Irene, too.

She allowed him his victory about leaving Barry, too. He was happy here. He'd settled in at Twelve Trees, their life in Vermont fading with each passing day.

A week later as she was leaving, Diana wondered how relaxing a weekend with Caleb could possibly be. She'd been ever watchful around him since she'd nearly given in to his lovemaking. It was almost as if she could no longer trust her perfidious body, which instinctively responded, allowing him to see she had needs. The incident had really shaken her. She wanted Caleb to declare himself. "It's only a matter of time," he'd said.

Lost in her thoughts, Diana became aware that Lottie was speaking to her. From the puzzled expression on her face Diana realized she must have been trying to get her attention for some time.

"I'm sorry, Lottie. What did you say? This heat has boiled my brain. I can't seem to concentrate."

"That's all right," Lottie answered shyly. "I just didn't want you worrying about Barry. Burtie and I will watch him every minute and Sterns is making arrangements to put a bed in the nursery I can sleep on. And if I take him to my house, all my family will help look out for him. I'll take good care of him." Having finished this carefully rehearsed little speech, Lottie hurried out, mumbling something about getting Barry and meeting her downstairs with him to say good-bye.

As soon as she'd left, Diana began searching through her closet, unbuttoning her blouse as she looked. Even with central air conditioning the mugginess seemed oppressive. Stripped of her blouse, she had tossed it on the bed when the door of the bedroom was suddenly thrust open and Caleb entered.

His eyes slowly traveled over her bare midriff, the flimsy bra allowing a tantalizing glimpse before she turned around searching quickly in the closet for something to wear.

"Is this all?" she heard him say. Out of the corner of her eye she saw him indicate the alligator suitcase.

"Yes. I can carry the cosmetic case myself." When he didn't make an effort to leave, she prompted, "Would you mind?"

"I do, rather. You have a beautiful body. It's only natural I like to look at my wife."

"Only look?" she taunted, with caustic sarcasm.

"There is nothing wrong with my libido. It's perfectly healthy." His eyes once again slowly traveled the length of her body. Her long honey-colored hair rested on her tanned shoulders. Her long legs were encased in Calvin Klein jeans, her slender feet in wedged-heeled sandals. She kept her arms crisscrossed in front.

With a toss of her head, Diana grabbed the first thing she saw—a sheer eyelet cotton blouse with a tie front. She quickly slipped it on. It was only as she started to turn around again that she saw his face reflected in the mirrored door of the closet, a gleam of amusement deep in his red-brown eyes.

"Would you mind taking your lustful gaze elsewhere? I'm sure you can find someone who would welcome it."

The statement seemed to anger him, his lips thinning, his voice short as he stated, "We'll be leaving in fifteen minutes."

An uncomfortable silence continued throughout the drive to Woodledge. The only break was the car radio and the hum of the climate control system, which kept the temperature cool and made the trip bearable.

Hartford to Woodledge wasn't far in mileage but back roads made the travel slow. Even so the drive seemed much shorter than when Diana had last come this way.

As the miles slipped by, the passing scenery made Diana grateful she'd remembered her camera. Picture taking could absorb hours of time, hours she'd need to spend avoiding Caleb. She wanted to capture a few shots of small woodland animals to show Barry. Wildlife flourished in the dense woods of Connecticut—red fox, rabbits, bushy-tailed squirrels, and a large variety of native birds and wildflowers.

Once past Winsted, Diana was grateful to see Platt Hill Drive and the clear waters of Highland Lake. In a few minutes more they would reach the turnoff to Woodledge. It would be nice to be away from the cool atmosphere that had prevailed inside the car since they'd left Twelve Trees.

Diana was grateful for one circumstance. Irene wasn't going with them. All the bedrooms at Woodledge were on the second floor. When Irene stated she would stay behind, Caleb hadn't protested, although Diana thought Irene had expected him to. Maybe he was tired of her self-pity. It could b wearisome.

Woodledge was nestled in a picturesque setting, surrounded by a wooded area and scrub oak. It was almost completely hidden from the road. Diana was having trouble forgetting her previous visit and it was with a certain anxiety and trepidation that she went inside. After greeting the caretaker and his wife, she followed Caleb up the circular stairway to the bedrooms above.

Diana managed to avoid glancing where she knew the library would be, although she was conscious of its whereabouts and the constant reminder of how much her presence in that room one night had changed her life.

At the first bedroom Caleb pushed open the door and deposited the bags just inside. Before turning away he said, his voice amused, "In case you have a reason for wanting to know, my bedroom is next door. Unless, of course, you'd prefer I stayed here."

Flushing under the dark gleam, she answered with a terse, "No, thanks."

In a softer voice he said, "Woodledge might be the best place to exorcise old ghosts. I could make you forget Barrett."

"No, you couldn't," she said sharply. She almost wanted to add, "because there are *no* ghosts to forget." It wasn't his brother she needed to dismiss from her mind, but Caleb himself. Not just their first meeting either, but the sensations she'd experienced that day he'd comforted her and it had ended with Caleb asking if he could stay. The shock those feelings had generated had never left. Never had she thought herself capable of such unbridled passion. She'd been totally oblivious to everything but Caleb that afternoon. She shook her head again. His eyes were dark, unreadable, his mouth grim. Diana caught a fleeting glimpse of hurt in his eyes before he shut the door with a sharp click.

Shaking her head, Diana decided she must have imagined it.

Caleb and Diana had to be civil to each other as their guests began arriving, first the Staffords, followed an hour later by Ben and Phyllis Martin. Ben was a board member at Buchanan's and he'd taken over Barrett's responsibilities upon his death.

The atmosphere was very relaxed and all the meals were informal, the idea being to rest and unwind from the heat and hectic city living. After dinner Phyllis suggested a walk and Diana agreed wholeheartedly. The brisk pace would be just the thing for Diana and she was grateful to Phyllis for suggesting it. It was ridiculous, of course, but she was avoiding the library.

Skirting the edge of the tennis court, they followed the same path Diana had taken two years previously. Moments later they crossed the dirt road—the exact place where she'd left her car. Her mind on the past, Diana stared at the spot.

A quail ended her reminiscing. All three of them jumped, startled as the bird darted from its hiding place. Camera in hand, Diana began snapping away, enjoying the diversion. At least for a few minutes her thoughts had an escape; they weren't on Caleb Buchanan or a dark, stormy night from out of her past. The library was the only place left that she had to avoid.

An hour later they came in the front door, laughing, exhilarated by the exercise. Tossing aside her sweater, Diana lagged behind the others as she watched the direction of their steps. She was close enough to hear Mildred's laughing comment. "This way, girls. I'd know Abe's cigar anywhere."

Diana glanced around the room, remembering. It was exactly as she recalled. At least the furniture seemed to be in the same place, which was all she really had perceived that dreadful night, that and the man on whom her eyes now focused. She stared at Caleb, seeing the enigmatic smile on his face as he sprawled in a deep chair, his eyes hooded as he watched her reaction.

For one infinitesimal second, horror and fear were

mirrored in her eyes as she valiantly tried to regain control.

"We'd have been back long ago, but our star photographer here insisted on taking pictures of everything that moved. . . ." Suddenly Phyllis noticed Diana's pallor.

"Diana, what's the matter? You're pale as a ghost," Phyllis said. "Are you ill?"

The question brought Diana out of her bad dream as she swallowed, her mouth dry, forcing her eyes away from Caleb's.

"Nothing. I'm just tired." She could hear the tremor in her voice. "I think I'll call it a day, if you don't mind my being rude. That walk has put me right out." When they all insisted it was fine, she murmured, "Goodnight, see you on the tennis court. Nine o'clock?"

The others nodded in agreement. She left without looking in Caleb's direction. She hadn't any desire to see his mocking smile again.

The sleep helped. It was easier the next day to confront the library, this time on her own. She'd been there a few minutes waiting for the others to come down, browsing through a selection of titles. Lifting her eyes, the air seemed to crackle with tension as she saw Caleb standing in the doorway.

"The caretaker's wife has a brunch ready, if you're through reliving old memories," Caleb said, his face a dark scowl. Undoubtedly he thought Diana was dwelling on remembrances of Barrett. Little could Caleb guess the only promptings this room invoked were dark thoughts of him. "The others are in the breakfast room," he added.

Without commenting, Diana followed him. It was easier in the presence of the others to act as if nothing was amiss between them.

"Mildred decided she preferred to sleep in," Abe

said, adding that his tennis days were behind him, too. "I've waited a long time just for the privilege of being old enough to watch others be energetic."

Diana soon found out how rusty she was. At one time she'd played avid tennis, and had even attended tennis camp the summer she was fourteen. One married couple pitted against the other soon proved a mismatch, so Phyllis and Diana switched places. Phyllis was Caleb's partner while Diana joined Ben's team.

It wasn't long before Diana began to feel the others didn't even exist. Deliberately she placed the return where it was necessary for Caleb to scramble to the opposite base line. Caleb was equally good at returning the favor. She found herself wishing she was in better shape.

Finally, Ben and Phyllis dropped out, leaving the other two to hash out a final set. The match quickly turned into a battle of wills. Caleb's physical endurance allowed him his victory in the end. As she began to tire, Diana sensed Caleb was merely playing a game of cat and mouse. She should have known better. She might be a pretty good player by most standards, but compared with Caleb, she was an amateur athlete.

Caleb hadn't even waited for her polite congratulations. She walked up to the net offering her hand. At the same time she pulled a band loose from her hair, allowing it to flow free, cascading over her shoulders, a honey-gold fire that caught the sunlight.

Ignoring the outstretched hand, he snapped, "Do something with that damn hair. It's all over the place."

Diana was taken aback by the totally unexpected anger.

It was Abe who came to Diana's defense, rejoining Caleb with, "My God, Caleb, you must be crazy. Her hair is gorgeous—the most beautiful hair I've ever seen."

Diana laughed. She was unsure what it was exactly about her hair that irritated Caleb so much, but she was grateful for any small way she could annoy him. "Honestly, Caleb, I just barely pulled it loose from the band. It happens to be hot. Anyone would think you lost the match instead of winning it. You're acting like Barry when he's missed his nap!"

He merely gave her a dark scowl before going inside.

After showering and changing their clothes, they climbed into the Staffords' Sedan de Ville and drove into Winsted for a pleasant lunch. After eating, they ventured the few miles to Riverton. Originally called Hitchcocks-ville, it was the home of the famous Hitchcock Chair Company. Many of the procedures were still practiced by hand in making the replicas of the rare nineteenth-century chair.

The three women lagged behind as the men strolled in the direction of the car. Handing a few bills to the clerk, Mildred commented on the factory tour. "It's amazing that we always play 'tourist' when we travel, but I've lived in Connecticut all my life and I'm ashamed to admit how little I know about my own state. Connecticut is so steeped in our nation's history, too."

"After that shopping spree, Abe is liable to nix any future explorations," Phyllis added with a laugh.

"Hopefully he won't find out. I had the purchases shipped."

They laughed, agreeing it was the wisest thing to do.

In returning to Woodledge, they took a different route. Crossing a bridge near the factory, they followed the Farmington River through People's State Forest. The trees beside the road were so tall and dense that they blocked the sunlight, making it seem more like dusk, instead of early afternoon.

When they'd returned to the car, Diana had found herself wedged between Caleb and Abe Stafford's portly frame. Caleb was driving. Because of Abe's bulk, she ended up in close quarters with Caleb, much closer than she liked. As they looked at each other, Diana saw the humorous glint deep in his eyes. He knew she was hating the closeness.

To allow more room for Abe's large frame, Diana placed her arm along the back of Caleb's seat and moved closer to him. From where her breast pressed against his shoulder to where thigh met thigh, Diana was conscious of one thing—Caleb. Once again, she found his amused gaze on her before his driving needed his attention. The contact with his warmed body confused her, made her want to move closer and farther away at the same time. The upturned corners of his mouth irritated her. Annoyed, Diana had the desire to wipe the smirk from his face.

Impulsively, she trailed the back of her hand along his cheek following the lean jawline. The skin felt raspy. The more relaxed atmosphere of Woodledge had allowed him to skip his usual shave that morning. She slipped her hand underneath his hair. Slowly, teasingly, she rubbed his neck, the reddish-brown thatch curled around her fingers. He wore it collar length.

Back and forth she stroked his neck.

When he glanced at her again the humor was gone. Caleb reached up and caught her hand in a hard grasp. He held it there in a bruising hold. His touch as well as the dark gaze sent sharp needle points along her fingertips where they came in contact with his skin. Although he didn't speak, the message was loud and clear. "Someday, someday. . . ."

Diana was grateful the others in the car didn't seem to think anything was amiss as they took a roundabout way of returning home, stopping in Litchfield. A town steeped in history, the old, well-tended colonial homes lined the streets adjacent to the village green. Litchfield, home of America's first law school, was preserved in detail. Even the grade books were available for inspection.

They paused to cool off with iced custards. When the confection melted on Diana's chin, Caleb wiped it away with a clean handkerchief from his pocket. He held her chin, making her look directly into his eyes. Her sensitive nerve endings tingled as he slowly brushed the soft cloth back and forth across her lips. The treatment was not unlike the way she'd rubbed his neck earlier. Diana was glad when they were back at Woodledge, out of the overly confining car.

A late-afternoon storm forced them to stay indoors as the sky darkened with threatening rain. Diana grimaced. Good Lord, even the weather conspired to recreate memories. Here they'd prayed for rain for a matter of weeks and now, when she could least appreciate the moisture, it fell.

Both the Martins and the Staffords were championship bridge players, each with master points to their credit, and it didn't take them long to find an answer to their enforced inactivity. Caleb soon appeared absorbed in a book, the stereo playing softly in the background. So Diana excused herself and went upstairs to take a nap. The drumming of the rain had the desired effect and she quickly fell asleep.

Diana wasn't sure how long she'd been asleep when she suddenly woke up. Attired in a lacy satin camisole, she yawned, loving the feel of the downy comforter beneath her body, relishing in the languor of half-sleep. She stretched like a kitten who had fallen asleep in the sun, lazily coming awake little by little. She rubbed her bare legs against the bedspread, enjoying the sensuous feel. She yawned, stretching again. The rain must have stopped, she thought, the air smelled dew-fresh, the aroma of spicy . . .

The grogginess suddenly disappeared and she opened her eyes.

Caleb stood at the foot of the bed. It had been the spicy smell of his aftershave that had shaken her from her slothful doze.

"I knocked."

"Why are you in here?" she said, her voice with a husky breathless quality. At the same time she began searching frantically for the light blanket she'd used as a cover.

"It's on the floor," he said, taking a couple of steps to where it lay beside the bed. Both of them reached down for it at the same time. Diana would have fallen if Caleb hadn't caught her arm, pushing her back with one hand, while at the same time he picked up the coverlet on the floor.

She jerked it back. As always, his touch caused sparks.

He never commented on her state of dress—or undress—as she expected him to, but merely said, his eyes unreadable, "You aren't going to like this, but Natalie Stafford arrived just now with her latest boyfriend in tow. I put him in my room. The only place left for Natalie was the sitting room in her parents' suite. The sofa makes into a bed."

Still groggy enough with sleep not to understand where the conversation was leading, she asked innocently, "Where will you sleep?"

"In here with you, darling wife!" he said, indicating the bags he'd already deposited by the door.

"No!" she said, her voice full of alarm. "You can't stay here."

"Sorry, but there isn't another bedroom!"

Grasping at straws she lashed out, her voice accusing, "You planned this, didn't you? By forcing me to spend the night in the same bed, you're hoping I'll find the circumstances too overwhelming to resist."

Her green eyes were luminous in the half light.

"Grow up, Diana. It's an unfortunate, unforeseeable turn of events. Delectable as your body is, I've never found it necessary to resort to force! I'm sure we can manage a couple of nights."

He turned and left.

She had put off going to bed as long as possible. Natalie had been quite willing to entertain them, swapping stories with her equally entertaining companion. Diana thought Natalie seemed to enjoy flirting outrageously with her boyfriend. Either she wanted Caleb's approval or she wanted to make him jealous. More than once her parents had referred to Nat's schoolgirl crush on Caleb. Evidently from his teasing attitude and the wry mobility of his mouth, Caleb, too, found it amusing.

One by one the others had drifted off until only Natalie and her boyfriend remained. Caleb said, looking at Diana, amusement in his voice, "I think we aren't wanted here. Go on up, darling." Then he added, his laughter even more apparent, "I'll be there as soon as I make sure the house is secure. No telling who might try and break in!"

Caleb walked meaningfully in the direction of the french doors.

He was so clever. At another time she might have taken the time to comment, but she had her reasons for wanting to hurry. She wanted to be in bed well before he got there and able to feign sleep when he arrived.

133

Her little pretense didn't fool him at all. Lying as close to the edge as was physically possible, she breathed quietly, rhythmically, grateful that the bed was extra-large.

It seemed to take forever for him to actually come to bed, and when at last she felt the opposite edge of the bed giving with his weight, she also heard his soft chuckle in the dark. "Be careful, Diana," Caleb said, his voice more amused than ever, "or you might fall off."

It had worked well the first night. Diana simply stayed awake most of the night to make sure that he kept his distance. The hours until dawn seemed endless. Hollow-eyed, she'd finally given up. Dressing in the bathroom, she'd left Caleb sleeping as peacefully as Barry, without a care in the world. He was sprawled across the bed, taking more than his fair share of it. His chest was bare down to where the sheet barely covered his lower half. She couldn't help but wonder if he had anything else on.

Plenty of exercise as well as the restless night had taken their toll and she went to bed the following night at an earlier hour. She vaguely recalled hearing Caleb climb under the covers, but remembered to keep her back turned well away from his side of the bed.

Lips were slowly tracing the outline of her mouth, a feather-soft touch. Deliciously sensual, a shaft of exquisite pleasure shot through her body making her want the dream to continue. A soft moan escaped her as the mouth became more insistent, probing the sweet moisture from within.

A warm hand caressed her, pushed aside her night-gown, touching the sleep-warm body, closing around

134

first one creamy breast, then another. Tantalizing, teasing in its slowness, the mouth followed the path the hands had just taken. The warm breath awakened sensitive nerve endings. The pulling touch of his mouth on her breast was ecstasy, making the tip a firm, hard bud.

She, too, had the urge to caress her dream lover. She moved one hand upward along his shoulder to be caught in his thick, unruly hair, while the other hand trailed slowly back and forth across his chest, loving the luxuriant feel of the curly mat under her palm, the hard nipples buried there. Her hand moved lower, following the line of hair that narrowed at his waist, then lower still, where her seeking fingers encountered a wide scar. She frowned in her sleep, trying to remember why it seemed so familiar?

She heard another low moan in the dark, this time from someone else! Her eyes flew open. She wasn't dreaming!

She pushed against the solid wall of Caleb's chest, horrified at what was happening, knowing she had been touching him.

"Caleb, stop!" she said, her voice breathless.

"I don't want to stop and neither do you!" he stated truthfully.

"You promised. You said you wouldn't use force!" she said, her hands locked in his hair, tugging with as much strength as she could find.

"Force. Hardly! Not when it was you who woke me! You curled up against me, running your hand up and down my spine. I can't resist that kind of temptation!"

"I must have been asleep." She couldn't believe she'd actually done it.

"Your body wasn't asleep," he said suggestively, his fingers brushing across the sensitive tip of her breast, pleased at the response he received. "Tell yourself all the lies you want, but don't try to make me believe them!"

His mouth once again claimed hers, probing, sending another sweet arrow of feeling along her spine.

With a strength born of fear, she shoved him away, bounding from the bed at the same time. She grabbed the robe that she had carefully laid out the night before. Quickly, she put it on. Desperately, she searched her mind for some way of making him stop, afraid of her own treacherous body.

Diana heard the rustle of bedclothes being tossed aside and knew he'd left the bed, intent on coaxing her to return. Hurriedly she crossed to the light and switched it on. The addition of stark reality to the emotion-packed room helped to dispel her temptation. But she could see from the dark look in his chestnut-brown eyes that he would not be deterred from his purpose. Grasping at straws, she said, her green eyes fearful, "I doubt very much Caleb that you'd want to make love to me in the same bed where Barry was conceived!" She watched a searing white anger cross his face. "Of course, I can't be a hundred percent sure . . . there were other places."

The wild look in his eyes told her she'd gone too far as fear of a different kind clutched at her. She cringed under the murderous intensity that replaced the wild look. He shook her like a rag doll, her head snapping with the force.

He continued, until he finally became conscious of his own violence. Throwing her across the bed, he grabbed his own robe and stormed out, slamming the door savagely behind him, uncaring that it was the middle of the night and there were other guests in the house.

How had she dared? She'd carried him to the absolute brink of insanity. He was like a volcano on the verge of a full-scale eruption. She was beginning tò wonder if she wasn't a little crazy herself.

It was a long night. Exhausted, she finally slept.

The next day he was barely civil to Diana. Their guests were well aware of underlying currents between the two of them. But it was only for Diana that he saved the acid politeness. She found this more scalding than any overt anger might have been. But even with the violence of the night before there was still one thing she had to do. She had to let him know she'd planned the whole thing as revenge for forcing her into an unwilling marriage, only the next time she would choose a place where her susceptibility wouldn't be so strong. At least she wouldn't be in the same bed with him!

Evidently he'd spent the remainder of the night in the library, and from his appearance the next day (and the fact he had a roaring headache), he'd obviously gotten royally drunk!

Later, as they and their guests were standing around their individual cars preparing to return to Hartford, Mildred asked about the Founder's Day dinner party, which was always held the first week of September. Caleb answered, saying, "Diana should have the invitations in the mail in a couple of weeks."

Now it was Diana's turn to stare blankly at him. She'd never heard of the fete. On the way to Hartford she asked him about it.

With the same chilly tone still apparent in his voice, he told her. The annual event had been started by his grandfather and it always followed Buchanan's largest auction of the year. Participants invited to Twelve Trees included executive directors of the company, art brokers and dealers, as well as close friends and neighbors.

"It is your responsibility as the mistress of Twelve Trees to plan the whole affair."

Caleb had loved adding this statement, fully aware of how much she hated this sort of party, especially one of this magnitude. She resorted to sarcasm. "Sort of 'an open palace for the royal subjects.' And since I'm the new Queen Bee, everyone is anxious to take a good look!"

Diana glanced at Caleb, saw the tight working of his jaw underneath the skin. But she continued, adding, "Why not have Irene plan it? She'd dearly love it and it would smooth matters over for leaving her home this weekend."

"We've been through this before, Diana. You'll take charge. You also know why she didn't go to Wood-ledge, too. All the bedrooms are on the second floor."

She couldn't refrain from taunting him. "You seemed to have managed rather well downstairs!" The laughter was apparent in her voice.

His voice was deadly. "One day, Diana, you'll go too far. You almost did last night. Never have I come so close to doing bodily harm to a woman—and to my own wife!"

There was a certain quality in his voice that made her cringe. But still wanting to have the last word, she added, clicking her tongue, "I'm scared to death."

False bravado. She wouldn't fare as well as she had last night if she dared to make him that angry again. These might just be her last words!

It was only as they neared home that Diana made a near-fatal comment. "A delightful weekend, Caleb. I do so hate to see it end." She added with sugary sweetness, "At least I'll soon be home to Barry. I can already hear his little crow of laughter. It always reminds me so much of Deanna."

"Who is Deanna?"

Diana felt grateful that he was driving. He wasn't able to see how much the question unnerved her. She was sure that if his dark gaze could look into her eyes, they would without doubt know something was amiss. She struggled to find an answer.

"She was a friend."

Chapter Ten

A couple of days before the Founders' Day party, Diana went into Hartford to pick up her new dress and take care of a few last-minute details for the party. She also intended to meet Steve and his girlfriend for a luncheon date. It was only as she parked the car that she remembered Caleb's edict of only seeing Steve at Twelve Trees. She felt a little shiver of fear before she lightly shrugged her shoulders.

Suzanne would be there too. Besides, once before she'd met Steve outside, although it had been unplanned. She'd taken Barry to the children's zoo and as they were returning home, Steve had seen the car at a stoplight and waved them over. They'd had an impromptu lunch at Honis's Oyster House, dining on the house specialty. Barry had tried to relate with his limited vocabulary his experiences with the pets at the zoo. The zoo's "hands-on" policy had delighted him— the visitors were actually encouraged to touch the animals.

Early for this luncheon appointment, it was nice to sit, relax and enjoy the view from the restaurant window. The past month had been hectic with the party preparations. The window overlooked Constitution Plaza, with the city below. The high-rise insurance office buildings seemed in contrast with the rounded dome of the centuries-old State Capitol building. This was the first of September and soon New England would have its autumn colors in magnificent array.

The wide span of the Connecticut River was visible from the window. It divided the east half of the state from the west—a well-traveled avenue used by the first settlers to the colonies. Because of its easy access, Hartford had become one of the busiest centers of trade, the city old before the Revolution, the highroad of history already imprinted on its back.

Diana loved the elm-and-oak-lined streets in the quaint little villages of her native state. If it hadn't been for the way she'd been forced to return, she wouldn't have minded moving back to Connecticut. She missed Marty, of course, and Jeff and the boys. Diana called often to chat, taking advantage of her affluent status to afford the long distant tolls to Vermont.

Diana glanced up from her musing to see Steve with a beautiful dark-haired girl, Suzanne. Introductions were made.

"Lovely," Diana murmured for Steve's ear alone. They followed closely behind Suzanne and the hostess as they maneuvered the way to their table.

"If I can't have you, babe," he bantered with an easy grin, "I guess I'll have to settle for second best."

Suzanne Webster was dressed in a yellow print sundress. The color of the dress was a nice foil for her shiny dark-brown hair, which moved freely on her shoulders. "Good figure, nice legs," Diana assessed. "Some second best!"

Steve grinned. "Yeh, it's rough!" Someone else must have agreed with him. They heard a low wolf whistle. Every male in the room glanced up and it wasn't until later that Diana learned that Caleb was among those in the dining room. The easygoing teasing between Steve and Diana didn't go unnoticed by him and the close proximity of their heads didn't either. Neither one noticed Caleb's presence. *Too wrapped up in themselves,* Caleb thought cynically. He would have been surprised if he could have heard their easy bantering, heard Steve continue, "As quickly as possible, I intend to put a ring on her finger. I've dilly-dallied around with cold feet long enough."

From the idolizing look on Suzanne's face, Diana doubted if he'd be turned down.

Once seated Steve asked, "How is the party progressing? Any hitches?"

"Two more days and I'll find out. Either it goes off smoothly or . . ."

"I'd be a bundle of nerves," Suzanne stated. "I couldn't even enjoy the party at all."

"You're a shy child," Steve said with a fond look in Suzanne's direction. "While Diana, here, could bluff her way out of any situation. She's a green-eyed cat with nine lives."

"I think I used up eight of them since I married Caleb Buchanan."

"Strictly from a male point of view, you probably earned every single one."

"Steven, I'm shocked," Diana said, a mild look of indignation on her face. "Much too male chauvinistic to come from my friend. You've been around Caleb too often."

He answered with his easy grin, "All right, to make amends and to show you I'm not just another pretty face, I'll come over the morning of the party and lend a helping hand."

"You're forgiven. Seriously, it has gone well—with only a few possible exceptions. The misplacment of the invitations was the only serious matter."

"Your sister-in-law?" Steve questioned.

Diana raised an expressive eyebrow. "How did you know?"

"Several times I've seen her look green with envy when she's with you."

As Steve and Suzanne placed their order for lunch, Diana's thoughts were riveted on Irene and the way she'd turned matters to her advantage after coaxing Diana into letting her help with the preparations for the party.

Diana would dearly have loved to tell Caleb that it was his "precious" Irene who had fouled up the invitations when she had insisted on doing her small part. Diana had ended up having to call all those invited to make sure they'd received their invitations. While she'd done the calling, Caleb had watched and listened, a dark scowl on his face.

Just once it would be nice to earn his approval, she thought, more hurt than she'd wanted to admit, even to herself. Her eyes felt hot and scratchy even thinking about the incident. *What's the matter with me,* she asked herself. *Good grief, Diana, you're not going to cry? Ridiculous, girl. Get hold of yourself before you do something foolish.* Resorting to tears wasn't her bag.

Diana came out of her reverie to see Steve and the waiter looking questioningly at her. Steve asked, evidently for the second time, "Is something the matter? He's waiting, Diana. Would you like to order?"

"Oh, I'm sorry. I was daydreaming. I'd like the red snapper, please."

Steve eyed her thoughtfully, but said nothing more about the pinched look on her face. The remainder of the meal passed uneventfully. Suzanne seemed to lose some of her shyness and began to participate in the conversation. Before they'd finished, she'd even let Diana see a glimpse of her wit, not unlike Steve's.

Neither Steve nor Diana noticed Caleb when he left.

As he had promised, Steve stopped by the day of the party to help with the last-minute details. Once they were finished, Diana had suggested they have a swim. With a hot noonday sun beaming down, Steve readily agreed.

They'd been in the water about half an hour when Caleb arrived home. Evidently he didn't think she could be trusted to organize the fete, and had decided to check if everything was ready. It had been unfortunate when he'd stepped outside and had found Diana purring as Steve applied suntan lotion to her back.

"Are you trying to get my eyes blackened?" Steve asked, hearing her throaty murmurs. Clean shaven, the mustache gone, his boyish grin seemed younger than ever.

She laughed, watching Caleb's approach through veiled lashes. "Would you go a round with him?"

"With that look on Caleb's face? No thanks. I have visions of living to a ripe old age. Married to Suzanne, children. Think of those as yet unnamed little kids, their father gone in his prime!"

They both had laughed but the sound had quickly died in Diana's throat as a shadow fell across their swimsuit-clad bodies.

"I'll finish that," Caleb said with cool politeness, a barely controlled quality in his voice as he continued by adding, "You have a phone call, Steve."

"Back in a sec. The office probably."

As soon as he was out of earshot, Diana said quickly, "You can stop now, Caleb. My back is fine. I don't need any more lotion. . . ." She started to sit up.

"Be still. Need it or not I'm going to finish this."

His touch was sensual. The lightest of caresses, making Diana hold her breath and grit her teeth. He stroked her back, his long fingers subtle, deliberately evasive. She wanted to scream, "Hurry up." The movement was tantalizingly slow. His voice was no longer cold. With a deeply resonant quality, he asked, "What are you thinking?" She shivered, but not from being cold as he traced a pattern in a zigzag motion down her spine. "What are you thinking, Diana?" he repeated, his voice soft, sexy . . . loverlike.

"Even my thoughts can't be my own."

His voice held real amusement. "Never mind. I already know what's bothering you. Here, let me," as she started to tie the strings of her bikini top. Finished, he brushed his lips across her shoulder.

"Caleb, stop!" Diana spun around, glaring at him, hating the sensations he was arousing, but especially hating the fact that he was doing it deliberately.

His eyes were dark, unreadable. "You are mine. I'll tolerate this game playing only so long. The ground rules might change if you step over the mark once too often."

He left.

Diana couldn't stand the tension anymore. Living under this strain was driving her slightly crazy. Surely soon he would take a stand. Then, and only then, could she say with the exact fervor she wanted, "Don't touch me, Caleb!"

Diana twirled in front of the mirror. The movement allowed the handkerchief hem of the dress to show a span of shapely leg before it settled once again. The muted print was exactly right—the lady at the dress salon had called it nymph green. Made of silk, it draped softly; the daring bodice required no bra and was held only by tiny straps.

Turning her head from side to side, she checked her makeup with critical eyes. Diana wanted to look her absolute best. She had never been vain about her good looks, but she wasn't unaware of them. How could she be? Men had made her conscious of her looks since she'd gotten through the awkward stage of age fifteen. Although it hadn't always proven a great asset, she was glad she was beautiful and shapely enough to at least cause Caleb a few sleepless nights.

Her skin, tanned to a golden honey, needed little makeup to improve its natural glow. Subtle smoky green eye shadow enhanced her eyes. It added to their depth, intensifying the green. Long dark lashes needed only a touch of mascara as she finished with a cinnamon-haze lipstick and an aromatic scent on her ear lobes and pulse points.

The toffee-rich sheen of her hair lay softly draped on her bare shoulders, one side pulled back with a dramatic flair by a tortoise-shell comb while the other side was full and free. The bright highlights in her hair created a gold fire as she moved. High-strapped sandals completed her appearance, her delicate arches and ankles almost bare.

The result was—she smiled, searching for a word— alluring, female, sexy possibly, but subtle and understated. Satisfied, she left to go downstairs, sure that she created just the effect she wanted.

Moments later the consequences of her careful grooming were reaffirmed when Caleb frowned on seeing her. His tall, well-built frame was stationed near the base of the stairs. Dressed superbly in a dinner jacket, silk shirt, and cummerbund, he greeted the earliest arrivals to their party.

Diana pirouetted, slowly turning for his approval, taunting softly, "Like it, darling?"

Richard Norris, who was among those just arriving,

responded before Caleb could. "Exquisite, my dear. I'd lock you up if you were mine."

The frown deepened.

"I think Caleb would prefer I was wearing a 'Mother Hubbard.' You'll really scowl, darling, when you get the bill."

Hard-corded muscles flexed under her hand as she slipped her hand under Caleb's arm. She knew if she continued with this constant mockery, she'd have to answer for the consequences.

"Keep it up, darling!" Caleb said, in a voice meant only for her ears. "Someday, if you continue to play the tune, you'll have to pay the piper."

"Really! I'm shaking with fear!"

"You should be," he finished, turning his attention to the last arrivals.

Among these happened to be Steve Brenner and with him, his girl, Suzanne Webster. She smiled shyly when introduced to the master of Twelve Trees. Caleb studied her with a long look before he glanced first at Steve, then at Diana. His dark eyes were unreadable. What was he thinking, Diana wondered?

Steve derided Caleb with, "All that brouhaha about my making a play for your wife was ridiculous, as you can see. My mind has been on other things," he admitted, smiling at Suzanne.

"You weren't the one trying to make me believe there was something going on." Dark eyes clashed with green, both aware who had done the baiting. "Diana has been nothing but a constant distraction," Caleb ventured, "since the day I married her."

"We could always get an annulment," Diana jeered softly, fully realizing the implication of this statement to anyone within earshot.

Diana watched Caleb's jaw clench and swallowed, knowing she'd gone too far.

His voice was dark with anger. "You finish here. I'll carry Irene from her room. She doesn't want to use her wheelchair tonight."

The words were terse and clipped, and Diana knew she hadn't heard the last of his wrath. She swallowed again. The moisture was gone from the inside of her mouth.

Diana continued talking to Steve and Suzanne, but part of her mind was on what the repercussions of the conversation would be. The velvet steel was back in Caleb's voice. He was livid, as he'd been that night at Woodledge. This time Diana wondered if she hadn't overstepped the boundary of no return. Would he forgive this latest indiscretion of her careless remark? During the remainder of the evening the cold fear stayed in the back of Diana's consciousness to return unbidden whenever she managed to catch his gaze.

The dinner was delicious. Burtie was a superior cook, but Diana felt a touch of pride that she had at least planned the menu—soup, followed by Dover sole in a creamy sauce, asparagus spears, crisp carrots, along with butterflake rolls, and chocolate mousse for dessert. Diana found she couldn't eat. She merely pushed the barely touched food around on her plate. Every once in a while she would catch Caleb's unfriendly glare, and it didn't prove beneficial to her digestion.

Irene proved to be a headache, too, with her sly remarks and innuendos all evening. Diana had almost reached the end of her tether, living in the same house with the woman. Irene couldn't be happy unless she and Caleb saw eye-to-eye on every blessed thing, and now, she was even beginning to interfere with Diana's raising of Barry. "He is totally uncontrollable," Irene had told Caleb, after Barry had broken her unicorn by accident.

Diana had wished she'd never taken Barry to see Irene. It was only after Irene had insisted a second time that Diana had relented. The last person she'd wanted to visit was Irene. She was positive Irene had distracted her deliberately, diverting her attention from Barry.

It had only taken a second and the priceless crystal unicorn was destroyed. Barry had toddled toward his mother, his hand outstretched, the object in two pieces.

"Oh no, not the unicorn. Caleb gave it to me. It's priceless." Irene's voice had grated. "I remember the broken cup and saucer. The child must be as awkward as his mother."

Diana had turned on her, frightening Irene with the fierce anger in her eyes, her tawny hair swinging wildly between them. Like a lioness defending her cub, she'd snapped, "No! You're not going to label him. That I won't stand for. Labels have a tendency to stick. We both know who broke the cup and saucer; as to the unicorn—you were supposed to be watching him, too. I can't see behind my back."

Diana had laid the broken pieces of the ornament on the coffee table. "You won't have to extend another invitation. We won't be back." She picked up Barry. "Don't worry, I won't tell Caleb about your behavior. We don't want to disillusion him, do we?"

The memory of Irene's face made Diana giggle. As she'd hurried out the door, she had heard Irene sputter before she finally said, "My behavior, you little snip! You've a nerve."

Surprisingly, Caleb hadn't been angry about the unicorn, only concerned if Barry had cut himself. He had told her to stay away from Irene, as though she needed a warning.

Even now, as Irene played through the intricacies of *Liebestraum*, Diana kept wishing she'd hit a discord, wondering how she could play so well and smile simperingly in Caleb's direction at the same time. At least Irene was trying her best to catch his eye.

Sour grapes, Diana thought, wondering what the matter was with her lately. Every time she saw the two of them together, she felt jealous. She must want his approval about something, just once. Then she remembered that she was on his blacklist again, if she had ever been off!

Absentmindedly, she ran her hand along the quilted brocade of the sofa, half listening to the music and Mr. Norris's occasional comments. But her thoughts were on the dark, brooding man who leaned with such casual elegance against the mantel. Her husband. It was funny how she was beginning to think of him in a totally different light. She'd lost the edge in this constant underlying warfare between them. Caleb Buchanan was a natural leader, one used to total command, and the few times she'd had an advantage over him, she knew he'd only tolerated it.

All evening it had been the same thing. Actually, his annoyance had begun with the incident at the pool earlier in the day. She'd known he was coming up the walk and had allowed Steve to continue rubbing the suntan lotion onto her back.

And now she had only added fuel to the fire with that remark in front of another man. It really didn't matter that Steve happened to be involved with another woman.

Surely Caleb would declare himself soon, and she could have the privilege of turning him down. This was her revenge for being forced into this unwilling marriage.

She glanced up, surprised to see him standing behind her. Warning bells rang at the dark look he gave her. She then followed his black glare. Mr. Norris's hand was resting on top of her own. She hadn't even noticed!

Surely Caleb couldn't be taking exception to that? It was completely innocent. She quickly removed her hand. Mr. Norris was a widower, true, but she was also a married woman. If Caleb wanted to be angry, she intended to make sure there were no halfway measures.

"Darling," she cooed softly, using her most seductive voice. "Won't you join us? We can make room here on the sofa, if you like." Diana patted the cushion beside herself, smiling up at Caleb with the full knowledge that from where he stood the alluring neckline of her dress allowed a complete vantage point, the rounded globes of her breasts easily discernible in the low light. She ran her fingertips lightly over the back of his hand, which rested casually next to her own.

The shock was instantaneous. Their touch always seemed to strike sparks. The dark hair on the back of his hand sent an electrical surge up her arm, making her tingle with awareness of him. Their eyes locked and held as his hand moved to enclose hers in a hard clasp.

They were the only two people in the room as far as they were concerned!

Mr. Norris noticed he was being ignored. His florid face lit up in a smile at the two of them. He commented, "Much as we are enjoying the recital, I think these two would prefer that we all just disappear. They are simply too polite to ask us to leave."

This remark brought an end to the party. Although there were protests, several of the guests began gathering their belongings and the party broke up. With the last departure, Diana began to help Sterns pick up the glasses and ashtrays. When she stacked the last of them on a tray, she bid Sterns a goodnight, telling him to leave everything else till morning.

Caleb carried Irene back to her suite and Diana had expected him to stay. Irene usually managed to keep him by making him feel guilty about her being an invalid. Diana had heard it so often she could easily recall that voice. She was surprised a moment later when she looked up to see Caleb standing in the doorway, that same formidable look on his features that had been there all evening.

Nervously, she fluffed cushions and straightened the already neat room.

"Leave it," he said. Some element in his speech increased her anxiety. In a voice that brooked no refusal, he said, "Come here."

"Would you care for a drink?" she asked, ignoring his command.

"I haven't had a drink all night! And I don't want one now. All I want is you! Come here," he repeated.

Not waiting for her to comply, he bridged the distance between them. Moments later he enclosed her in the hard circle of his arms, his lips on hers, drawing the very essence from her. It agitated her to know that even though she was angered by his arrogant attitude, his mouth could still arouse her so much. Unwillingly she became a participant. He cupped his hand around her throat, his thumb brushing the pulse point visible there, betraying the rapid beat of her heart.

Her lips clung to his, having a will of their own under the ardor of his desire-inducing kiss. He moved to slide the straps of the gown down from her shoulders, this bringing only a slight protest from her. She was so drugged by the sensations that filled her, she was putty in his hands. His lips had left hers, and were brushing the tops of her breasts. They ached for his touch, swelling as he cupped them in the palm of his hand.

The need to surrender invaded her whole body, the warmth of desire enervating as it traveled to every sensitive nerve ending in her body. Diana trembled with these new sensations. An ever-changing array of feelings swept through her and she knew this must stop. It was now or never.

"You want me," she coaxed, already knowing the answer.

"Yes." A statement of fact.

"I'm glad, Caleb," she said softly, meaningfully, "because this is as far as it goes. Unless you intend to use force."

His eyes locked with hers as he realized she'd done this intentionally.

"You did this deliberately."

"What a good guess. I've finally found your Achilles' heel, Caleb. I hope you ache all night long with desire. It took me a while to pay in full, but it was worth it to know I've thwarted you in a very personal way."

With this she turned and went upstairs, leaving Caleb with a black look of anger on his face. A few minutes later when she shut the door of her room and leaned against it, she wondered why she felt no sense of triumph.

For months she had planned her reprisal, but somehow she felt not the victor, but the loser. Her hands still trembled as she unzipped the dress, letting it fall at her feet with her slip, then kicked off her shoes and panty hose with the next motion.

Naked, she caught sight of her body in the full-length mirror. She hadn't bothered with the light, but even in the darkened room she knew there were changes and her skin tingled as she slowly ran her hands over her body, pretending they were Caleb's arms as they came up to cup the swelling softness of her breasts. She wanted him to see her like this, to finish what she'd started tonight. How well she remembered the throbbing ache that had traveled through her.

You, Diana, have been caught in a trap of your own

making. There was no victory in knowing Caleb wanted her too.

Disgusted by having to admit this and feeling slightly ridiculous standing there nude, gazing at her own image, she went to draw a hot bath. Maybe that would help her relax.

An hour later she still had slept little. She turned on the light. The bedside alarm clock indicated two o'clock. What was the matter with her? She knew the answer. She'd fallen in love with her *own* husband. At least her limited knowledge of the condition made her believe she was a victim. She wanted him. As husband and wife, she wanted his love.

She sat up, swinging her legs to the floor. Unsure what her exact intentions were, she walked to the sliding door and pushed it aside. The cool night air touched her heated skin through the sheer fabric of her nightgown. She lifted her long hair away from the nape of her neck, allowing the night breeze to caress her skin.

Diana wanted Caleb, and only one thing held her back. If he took her, he'd know Barry wasn't her child. It was the one and only factor that kept her from going to his room. Once there she knew exactly what her instinct would prompt her to do.

"Caleb," she would call softly. He would sit up in bed, immediately awake. Nothing else would need to be said. She'd untie the strings at her shoulders and slowly the gown would fall. She could picture his eyes. . . .

Stop it, Diana, she chided herself. *You're crazy, letting your thoughts run rampant. The next thing you know you will go to him.* This she knew was impossible. She couldn't.

She told herself to go check on Barry. *Take some aspirin, a cold shower, anything—only forget Caleb!*

Chapter Eleven

Diana walked quietly along the balcony to the next room. Pushing aside the door she stepped inside Barry's room. She found him asleep in a disarray of stuffed animals, huddled in a small ball, his arms tucked underneath him, his little pajama-clad bottom high in the air. She covered him with a light blanket taking a few minutes to straighten the room.

As she stepped back onto the balcony she glanced up to see Caleb standing in front of her, a brown robe knotted carelessly around his waist, his dark brown hair unruly, still damp from a shower. The russet-brown hair on his chest was visible through the opening in the robe. In his hand he held a glass half full of liquid.

Diana felt the warmth that invaded her cheeks as his eyes slid boldly over her, taking in her appearance with an all-consuming glance. She knew without looking what he saw—hair in rather wild abandon about her shoulders, the plunging line of her nightgown revealing more than it concealed.

"Let me by," she snapped.

With a rather exaggerated bow he allowed her to continue on along the balcony. But as she turned to shut the door, Diana was shocked to find he had followed her into the room. Caleb shut the door with a resounding click.

"Get out," she said, her voice tremulous despite her valiant effort to control it.

"Not yet." He spoke softly, a wealth of meaning in his voice as he set the glass down on the table beside the bed. "After tonight an annulment will be out of the question."

"You're drunk!" she stated. Her panic began to take effect as she watched him click off the bedside lamp. As he approached, she quickly backed away.

"Hardly! Two drinks wouldn't make me insensible." His white teeth flashed, easily discernible in the bright moonlight that filtered through the windows. Though his lips turned up with a cynical twist, the deep darkening color of his eyes was without laughter as he added, "Would you care for a drink? It would help you to relax."

His voice was quiet, unrelenting. A sudden unreasoning apprehension filled her as she guessed his intentions.

"Caleb, there are matters you don't understand. We have to talk," she whispered, her voice taut with fear.

"The time for talking is over, Diana."

As he reached out, she swung wildly trying desperately to get away. With a muffled oath he easily caught her flailing arms, in no way a match for the muscled strength of his own. He held her effortlessly with one hand, pulling the strings at her shoulders. With a single fluid motion, her gown fell.

"You're not teasing some besotted middle-aged man or beardless boy," he stated, holding her easily, his voice husky with desire as his eyes slid boldly over her contours, his hand catching in her hair making her look directly at him and the darkening look in his eyes. Startled, she felt his hand cup the soft roundness of her breast as she was held firmly against him.

"Are you ready to admit you want me as much as I want you?"

"No!" she gasped, frightened, trying unsuccessfully again to get away.

He merely tightened the hold in her hair.

"Okay, have it your way, wildcat," he rasped. Panting with the exertion, he swung her into his arms and deposited her roughly on the bed.

Before she had a chance to roll away, he divested himself of his robe and was beside her, trapping her beneath his leg and shoulder, his one hand free to slide boldly over her hip and thigh. He lowered his head. His lips parted hers as he kissed her long and deep. Tears of frustration welled in her eyes as she fought against the lethargy invading her body, the wild impulse to surrender under the primitive aching need beginning to assert itself. With frantic despair she felt his breath searing her skin as it trailed from the corner of her mouth, down the smooth column of her throat, then even lower to the valley between her breasts. She gasped as his lips traveled to one sensitive peak. "Please, don't!"

She brought up her free hand, flailed at him, tears of panic overflowing in wet tracks down her cheeks. He shifted, unmoved by her tears, to press against the entire length of her body. She still resisted as he pulled her roughly to him, their bodies at last fitted together in an inescapable bond.

An oath of surprise escaped his lips. Her luminous green eyes opened to stare into the velvet blackness of his gaze as his eyes registered incredible disbelief.

Endlessly, the look continued. Slowly he lowered his head, caressing the taut cords of her neck, whispering words of reassurance against her ear, willing her to relax. Unwillingly her body betrayed her. She felt the rising surrender, the bittersweet taste of passion well up

in her despite her denouncement of its existence in this
rapacious scene. The scent of spicy aftershave mixed
with the heat of their bodies assaulted her senses. A
painful fullness filled her, moving like warm honey
through her loins, a fullness that ached for assuage-
ment, sweet release. He seemed to hold her on a
distant threshold, expertly waiting, his own longing and
need keenly betrayed by the rapid beat of his heart
against her breast, the panting breath that fanned her
cheek.

A final whimper escaped her lips. "Please," she
whispered, till even he could wait no longer.

Much later Caleb rolled away, pulling the sheet
across him, reaching at the same time for the light
switch on the bedside table.

"Please . . . no!" she pleaded in an anguished whisper as she guessed his intentions. But almost before the
words were spoken, the room was bathed in the soft
glow of the night light.

Caleb turned toward her, ignoring the plea. His
dark, ominous gaze studied her, taking in with an
all-encompassing glance the rumpled, stained bed, the
tear-streaked face, the tawny-tangled halo of hair, wild
as it cascaded around her shoulders, the sheen and
silken afterglow of her body before she quickly covered
it with the sheet.

Disbelief still alive in his eyes, he questioned her.
"Okay, green eyes, I'd like a few answers." His hand
caught her chin and forced her to look at him.

She knocked his hand away, green fire leveled in his
direction, the anger beginning to return.

"Leave me alone. Haven't you done enough?"

He leaned over her, his grip a bruising hold on her
shoulder as he forced her to look at him.

"Be fair, Diana. This isn't all my doing. Kept in the dark about certain things, how was I to know . . ."

". . . that I wasn't fair game," she interrupted and finished for him.

". . . that you aren't Barry's mother. That before tonight you've never known a man. Why the lies?"

Diana merely glared with bitter contempt at the man who had initiated her body into intimacy, the same body that had betrayed her before it was over.

"I'm still waiting," he said in an inflexible voice. "Who is Barry's mother?"

"Does it matter? He's been mine since he was born."

"It matters. The whole story, Diana. Out with it." His meaning was clear as he added in a voice that brooked no refusal, "You'll stay right where you are—just as you are—until you do!"

Diana knew he meant what he said. She began in a husky whisper. "My sister, Deanna, was Barry's mother. She was ill and it upset her to have those letters, her love letters to your brother, read by just anyone. Besides, she was afraid you'd read about the baby she expected, afraid you'd try to take him away."

"Why didn't you tell the truth? Why pretend to be someone else that night?"

"Why?" she shrugged lightly, staring at the ceiling, remembering. "It didn't seem important enough at the time to correct your mistake. I didn't intend to ever see you again. We were going away as soon as the baby was born." Impatiently Diana paused to brush away the salty tears that kept forming of their own volition. She continued, "Only Deanna died when he was born and I'd promised her I'd leave Hartford. She was afraid for Barry."

"You could have told me the truth when we met again. Later, when I insisted we marry," he inserted.

"You threatened to take Barry from me, remember? The relationship was the same—aunt against uncle, and with you holding the trump card, money! 'No expense spared' you said. As long as you thought I was his natural mother, I was in a much better position to fight you. I moved to Vermont following Dee's death and everyone there took it for granted that I was Barry's mother. I never disputed it. End of story. Now will you go?"

"Whatever the reason fate had for bringing us together, Barry is where he belongs. Everything that would have been Barrett's will be his son's. This house . . ."

"He had a house—not just a house, a home! A bit more humble than this, true, but we were happy. Why couldn't you have just left us alone, me alone!" she added vehemently, sitting up and pulling the sheet with the motion.

"Diana," he said, his voice husky, affected as always by her thick toffee-colored head of gold. "What happened tonight was inevitable, and," he added as he watched for her reaction, "not totally of my instigation!"

"Oh sure! I dragged you in here!" Her voice was full of sarcasm.

His hand pushed back her hair, lingering in its silky tresses. "Blame me if you must," he ventured, "but we both know the truth, don't we? Don't we?" he insisted, his hand caught cruelly in her hair, forcing her to look at him.

Caleb didn't wait for an admission; he knew she understood what he stated so forcefully. "We both wanted this. Denying it won't make any difference. If you hadn't been afraid of what a night in my arms would reveal, what happened tonight would have happened a lot sooner. You've known how much I've wanted you and you've used that knowledge to punish me for forcing you into an unwilling marriage. Admit it," he insisted.

Mesmerized, they stared at each other. Neither was willing to confess to the other the full extent of their attraction. There was an alive awareness between them that they were just beginning to reveal, even to themselves.

"Okay, green eyes, there is one way we can communicate. I want to feel you melt beneath me again."

Diana swallowed, warmth invading her face. His eyes were dark pools of desire, reflective. She murmured a slight protest, having a certain reluctance as she guessed his intentions, wanting him to stop and continue at one and the same time. He stood, reaching out, his hand touched hers where she clasped the sheet against her breasts. Never taking his eyes from hers, she allowed him to loosen her fingers, pulling them away one by one, and the sheet slowly fell.

As the cool night air touched her skin, she watched his eyes intensifying to the deepest, darkest brown, alive with burning need.

"You are so beautiful," he whispered.

The look on his face sent a shiver of anticipation along her spine. For the first time since he'd turned on the light, her eyes left his face and she looked at his body. Innocent of ever having seen a man unclothed, she nonetheless couldn't keep from boldly allowing her gaze to travel lingeringly down his muscled length. He bent. There was the slight sound as the sheet was tossed aside.

Then his insistent mouth covered hers, his thrusting tongue simulating his need, making her fully realize how intimate and arousing the touch of mouth upon mouth can be. With a will of their own, her hands came up to run through the thick thatch of his hair.

Softly, teasingly, he caressed her. He touched her body, lightly running his hands over her like a whisper-soft breath. Hot tingles ran through her body, treacherously giving him the response he wanted. She was intensely aware of Caleb's body, the toned muscles and the clean lines of his physique. From deep within came the strongest primeval urge to be possessed again by him. She felt tinglingly alive, her senses at their keenest.

"Are you going to admit it?" he asked, completely in control, waiting for an answer.

"Yes," she whispered, giving him his victory.

"You were meant to be loved by me." Then he added, elation in his voice, remembering, "and *only* me." Smiling down at her as she lay in his arms, Caleb lifted a tawny golden strand of hair, its silky texture curling around his finger. "I waited so long to make you mine. It seemed like forever." He kissed her fiercely, hurting at first, then softened his caress as he said against her mouth, "You've driven me frenzied with need—and deliberately, too. There were times I could have cheerfully wrung your neck!"

The warmth of desire was like sweet wild honey as it traveled slowly through her, leaving her aching with awareness of him.

"Look at us, Di. Don't we fit together perfectly." The palm of his hand moved back and forth across the sensitized tip of her breast, turning it into a hard bud of desire.

"Diana," he begged, his voice a husky moan.

Traveling slowly downward with her hands, she held him tightly against her and entreated him not to linger. Diana reveled in the low groan of pleasure that escaped his mouth, enjoying her capacity to make him react that way. But even so she was fully cognizant of the fact that he possessed the same sort of hold over her. She could feel the muscles of his back knot with tension as a fog of longing began to envelop both of them.

Diana was awakened by a warm hand on her shoulder. A dark head was barely visible in the faint light of daybreak. The head leaned closer as a deep male voice whispered, "Good morning."

For one startled moment she stared. Then memories of the night before came rushing back and her face warmed under his intimate, penetrating look. Amusement followed his intense gaze as she brushed the hair from her eyes. Shy about their new intimacy, Diana hastily tugged the sheet in place, holding it down with her arms.

She felt his hand lift her chin. He kissed her. A brief kiss, but with promise of tenderness and passion to come.

"Come run with me, Diana. Let me show you the best time of the day."

"At this hour? And what about Barry?"

"I'll go turn on his intercom. Sterns rises early. He can listen for him." Caleb rose to leave. Shy again at the intimacy they'd shared, she kept her eyes averted from his naked body as he added with wry amusement, "This time I'll leave you to dress in private, otherwise we might miss our run. Hurry up, I'll give you half an hour." He left.

She used half of her allotted time taking a quick shower, aware as she washed her body of the changes last night's lovemaking had evoked. Never in her wildest imagination had she ever conceived what mindless blissful contentment could happen between a man and a woman. Would Caleb tell her he loved her now? That it wasn't only desire that motivated him?

Not wanting Caleb to arrive back too soon, Diana hurriedly dressed in jogging shorts, T-shirt, and running shoes. She was just tying the laces when Caleb pushed open the door. When he saw she was dressed, he said, amused, "I was hoping you'd dally along."

Taking her hand, he pulled her outside into the dew-fresh morning, the light of a new day beginning to break in the east. As she inhaled the sweet freshness, Diana felt vital, alive! A new day, a new life. As they reached the track, Caleb's smile told Diana he felt the same way.

It was ridiculous, of course. There wasn't any way she could keep up with him. Caleb was a marathon jogger. After only a few minutes she felt as if she'd been running for hours and Caleb wasn't even breathing deeply.

"I can't do this," she gasped. "I'm completely out of shape."

"Not completely!" he said with a grin as Diana was allowed to see a different side of Caleb, a teasing, fun-loving side. She liked this humorous, earthy, less-inhibited mate. Maybe they could make their marriage work, could find some meaning to this marriage after its dreadful beginning.

Last night she had admitted, if only to herself, how much she loved him. But all that had been revealed between the two of them was their overwhelming physical attraction. Both of them had been burned once. Burtie had told her how Caleb had been hurt first by the defection of his mother, at seventeen, followed by a love affair that had gone wrong when he was in his early twenties. It gave credence to a fact that Diana had long suspected—Caleb was as vulnerable as she was afraid of making commitments. Thank goodness that stupid girl had thrown Caleb over for someone else. She hadn't been too smart if she wasn't able to realize he was a man of principle and integrity, and, underneath the velvet steel, a tender, passionate lover.

Although she couldn't be completely sure, Diana was almost certain he'd been faithful, kept his vows to her even though their marriage had been in name only. Suddenly she was glad she'd been innocent, knowing that had pleased Caleb. Her face warmed, remembering, even without any previous knowledge to rely on, that Caleb was a superb lover. A slow, tingling sensation traveled along her spine anticipating the next time.

This was their beginning, a starting place to begin building a successful marriage.

"Caleb . . . I have to stop. There's a stitch in my side," she panted, straining to get the words out.

Exhibiting no exertion at all, he grinned, "Why we've scarcely come a mile."

"I'll wait here," Diana said, gesturing toward the summerhouse. "If I rest long enough I can make it back home today."

"Maybe I should rest, too. Suddenly a great weariness has come over me."

Diana could feel her heartbeat slow under the exertion, then begin to beat faster under the look in his eye. Caleb led her into the gazebo, made a bed of the bench cushions, and covered them with the beach towels he found inside the benches. When he was finished, he encouraged her to rest. "Catch your breath."

It was funny how relaxed, how natural it seemed. He was going to make love to her again. She knew it, but most of the shyness was gone this time. . . .

* * *

An hour later they walked back, hand in hand. As they neared the entrance to Twelve Trees, she asked him, "How do I look?" Diana felt sure the whole world could guess what they had been doing.

"Except for a delightful, tousled look, and a smudge on the end of your nose, nobody will know."

"I bet it's not the only smudge I have," she said pertly.

Caleb grinned. "Undoubtedly, but it won't show!" They both laughed.

Chapter Twelve

Weeks later Diana would always look back on this good beginning and wonder where it had gone wrong. Perhaps if there had been fewer "ifs"—if they'd been more sure of each other, if their past experiences hadn't served to remind them of the unfaithfulness of the opposite sex, and if Irene hadn't been living with them, there to see their happiness and begin to undermine it before it could take firm roots.

As casually as possible, Diana had suggested Irene might live elsewhere. "There isn't any reason Irene couldn't have her own place, is there? It's always been said two women couldn't live in the same house," Diana said, adding with her own thoughts, *wanting the same man!* Her voice had a lightness she really didn't feel.

"Diana," Caleb stated, "you have to see, my hands are tied. She was Barrett's wife, I can't ask her to leave. What I happen to want doesn't apply."

"I'm your wife, Caleb. What about me? My needs? It just isn't working with the two of us in the same house."

"As long as she wants to stay, Diana, she can. That is the last word I will say on the subject."

"The last decree, you mean!"

At first their quarrels had ended in their own special torment. A different kind of lovemaking. But finally the knowledge dawned on Diana that if she were to keep a portion of her soul to call her own, she must make him realize what he was doing. If only there had been some admission of love from him. Their compatibility in the bedroom wasn't the only basis of a good marriage.

Caleb couldn't begin to guess at all the "little things" Irene did to manipulate people. She was extremely clever. It was easy to see the traps she set, after the deed. Hindsight is always better than foresight! And Irene was very careful, at least when Caleb was near.

Somehow Irene had guessed about Barrett's being Barry's true father. When Irene asked Diana about it, she'd caught Diana completely unawares, exactly as she intended to.

Irene had been arranging some flowers, waiting for some friends to arrive from New York. She looked up from the flowers and asked quite casually, "Barrett was Barry's father, wasn't he?"

Diana had been setting the table for the evening meal. She just stood there dumbfounded with the silverware in her hand, unsure what to say, she'd been taken so completely by surprise.

"You needn't take the time to think up an answer. I already know the truth," Irene added, her eyes cold. "Why couldn't you leave him alone? Why Caleb, too? Wasn't one brother enough?" Her eyes were now venomous as she continued, "As I told you, it was always Caleb I wanted, first and foremost. Barrett was second choice. Whatever it takes, I'll have Caleb too one day soon."

Diana finally found her silent tongue.

"He happens to be married to me. What makes you

think he'll want you when he finds out how you duped him?"

"What do you mean?"

"The fact that you can walk!" Diana stated, watching the reaction.

"Oh!" Irene said, surprise in her pale blue eyes. "You know about that, do you? So we each know the other's little secret. I'm warning you, Diana dear, you are way out of your league. I'll use any advantage I can find to have Caleb. I will have him in the end."

"The irony is that not very long ago, I couldn't have cared less!" Diana laughed. "But now, Irene dear, I'll give you a good run for the prize. In this case, Caleb."

"I can't believe how naive you are. You can't actually believe I'd let you win." Her laugh was cruel. "There is something perhaps you should know. I was driving the night Barrett was killed—I deliberately ran the car off the road." Her blue eyes hard, Irene watched Diana's shocked expression of disbelief. She continued sotto voce, "I can't say what exactly my reasons were. Barrett intended to leave me. He also threatened to tell Caleb everything about the sham our marriage really was. That I couldn't allow. The embankment was steep, but not necessarily life-threatening—only I happened to be wearing a seat belt and Barrett wasn't. He was thrown from the car." Her blue eyes were as dark as night. "My legs were without feeling at first. But gradually, over the past year, they've gotten better. I kept the knowledge to myself."

"Did you know Barrett tried to give you a touching little message the night he died? I heard the ambulance attendant tell him he would see it was delivered before they took me away."

"Yes, I got it," Diana whispered, so affected by Irene's words that she could barely speak. She didn't enlighten Irene that the message had been for her sister, or that the message hadn't made any sense.

"You know, of course, if you tell any of this to Caleb, I'll deny it!"

"Caleb won't believe you," Diana said, sure it was true. Diana failed to see Irene's look or realize how devious and ambitious Irene really was.

"We'll see." A thoughtful look came into Irene's eyes, as she added softly, almost to herself, "We'll see."

Diana was well aware that Irene had spoken the truth when she said Diana was way out of her league. She also thought she knew Caleb well enough to think he would believe her before Irene.

Irene hadn't waited for him to come home. She had called Caleb at work in a hysterical, tear-filled voice pleading with him to "Please come home! Something has happened!"

It was later that Diana had seen how clever Irene could be.

Two hours after his arrival home Caleb came to see Diana, finding her alone in the bedroom they now shared. She'd just taken a bath and had washed her hair. Barefoot, with Caleb towering over her, Diana felt small and vulnerable. Rubbing her damp hair absentmindedly with a towel, she couldn't believe his next words.

"I told you I needed your help, how my hands were tied. Why did you do it?"

"Do what?" Diana asked, puzzled, sensing his anger. She hadn't a clue as to what he was talking about.

"Are you going to deny you told Irene who Barry's real father is?"

"Well, no. Not exactly," Diana corrected. "She asked me. . . ."

". . . and you couldn't wait to let her know the truth! You want her out of the house, and what better way than letting her see what a painful reminder Barry will be every day. Very clever, Diana."

"It wasn't that way at all. Let me . . ."

"I've already seen. She is almost hysterical. Her eyes are swollen shut from crying. She could hardly talk when she called me at Buchanan's. There are dinner guests from New York, friends of hers. I had to tell them she'd had an upset, that she refused to see them. You know how much she loves company."

"Caleb, be fair. No matter how it looks, none of this was deliberate, at least on my part." Even now she wanted him to see without implicating Irene's scheme. "Think. Is this really something I would do? Deliberately? Would I really set out just to hurt Irene by telling her about Barry? Am I really capable of that kind of deception?"

Caleb passed his hand wearily over his eyes.

"Who knows how the deceitful female mind works? Maybe you wanted to extract some revenge for the pain Irene caused your sister. Maybe you merely wanted her away from Twelve Trees. Maybe it was jealousy. Irene said she told you about her feelings about . . . me. Was that it?"

Diana took refuge behind biting sarcasm, afraid otherwise he'd see how cutting his words were, afraid he'd guess the truth about her feelings.

"Very conceited of you, Caleb. Jealousy is only an emotion that happens when the person involved is in love!" Diana stated, her voice hollow. "Since I haven't admitted to any such state, it would be highly unlikely."

His eyes were unreadable behind his dark stare as he digested her words. "You don't deny any of the things I've just said."

"Would it do any good? You've already tried and convicted me." Suddenly Diana felt a bone-weary tiredness, an unusual sensation when she had been verbally sparring with Caleb. Normally it was invigorating, with a revival of renewed energy, making her sharp, searching for a witty retort. Now she only felt exhausted.

There was another unusual sensation that was also extremely rare for Diana. A prickly feeling was behind her eyes. She wanted—needed—to cry, unbelievable as it seemed.

She prayed he'd soon leave, in case it happened to be true.

"Would you mind leaving? I'm sure Irene needs you. I certainly don't."

Anger still deep in his dark eyes, he turned and left.

Later that same evening, he'd returned to their bedroom. Evidently with some change of heart, he thought he might possibly be partially in the wrong and wanted to settle their differences. But, self-righteously, still hurt by his callous words, Diana had rejected his offer.

"Diana, we are adults," he persisted. "Irene made everything so plausible . . . I listened, surely that is understandable. My words were hasty. I'm sorry."

He stepped toward her as though to pull her close. Afraid of her own weak-willed body where Caleb was concerned, she lashed out, pushing him away.

"Don't touch me!"

The words were harsh, more brusque than she had intended. If only he'd made some verbal commitment that he loved her as well—that there was more to their marriage than how well-matched they were in bed.

Caleb saw only that she refused.

"All right, Diana," Caleb said, his voice sounding weary. "I'd like to be greeted when I come home at night by a warm, affectionate wife instead of a snarling witch. I'll not touch you until you ask."

"You think it keeps me humble to have to ask. I won't."

"Have it your way." He turned and abruptly left the room.

Diana couldn't believe the coldness she'd seen in his eyes, not after the warmth she'd seen so many times before. It was shattering to have him look at her without any feeling. She wanted to call him back, wishing she could take back the angry words.

She'd undressed and slipped between the sheets, half expecting him to relent, come to her bed—the bed they'd been sharing for the last few weeks. She wanted to have him pull her close within the circle of his arms.

It was only as she woke after her restless night that she knew he'd taken her at her word. It was the first time she'd slept alone since their marriage had become a real one. Heavy-hearted, Diana went downstairs, hoping to have some word with Caleb. It was early, she'd catch him before he left for Buchanan's. Maybe if she admitted to being a bit mule-headed he'd laugh, the warmth coming back into his eyes again, and they'd go back upstairs.

Delving into this fantasy, she was rudely awakened from her reverie. Burtie declared, as Diana came into the kitchen, "He's gone. He left an hour ago." Her voice accusing, she added, "You are quarreling with him."

"It does take two, Burtie," Diana answered back sharply, feeling a flare of anger. Burtie always managed to see his side of things. It was quickly amended a few moments later. Diana felt a surge of guilt when Burtie added, in a tone that clearly said she was disgusted with them both, "I've washed my hands of the two of you. Neither one of you can see the forest for the trees."

Diana couldn't help but agree. Barry sometimes used more logic than she and Caleb did.

It was only later in the afternoon that Diana learned from Irene that Caleb intended to be gone for several days. He was flying to London. Diana wasn't to know he'd given the message to Irene because his plane was departing immediately. He also had said to tell Diana that they'd talk as soon as he was back: it was a slight omission on Irene's part. She merely forgot to pass the message on.

Diana was unable to hide her astonishment from Irene. With a triumphant little smile, Irene's blue eyes held a cold gleam, enjoying the hurt in Diana's eyes. "You can see he's tired of you . . . you're the toy who is out of favor. Run back to Vermont. Take your paints, blue jeans, and schoolgirl ways. Twelve Trees needs a woman as its mistress. When Caleb knows I can walk . . . knows I can give him a son . . . it will be me he wants."

Shaking her head, Diana couldn't believe it. Surely, after all they'd been to each other—to leave without even a word of good-bye? Could the things Irene said be true?

A week later, on the day of his return, Diana was beginning to realize they were true. She had to leave while she still could. *Before you can't give him up*, she told herself, wondering if it wasn't already too late. A short time later she had her answer. An overheard conversation made her realize the fact that Irene spoke the truth.

She'd been in the library, lying on the cushioned window seat, reading. Tired, she must have dozed, the result of her restless, sleepless nights. It was some time later when she was startled from a deep sleep. The first voice she heard was Irene's.

"Caleb, be careful. You're spilling your coffee!"

Below the open window, Diana could see the two of them, seated at one of the patio tables by the swimming pool. She listened, their voices easily carrying to where she sat.

"Irene," Caleb said, his voice full of wonder, "I think you moved your leg. I'm sure you jerked it, trying to avoid the hot liquid!"

Caleb stared at Irene. Moments passed, then slowly he smiled.

"Irene," he continued, "do you realize what it could mean if it's true! You might be able to walk, have a normal life!"

Mesmerized Diana watched Caleb bend over Irene, his head close to her smooth blonde hair, which was in total contrast with his dark unruly one.

"It's not just a possibility, Caleb," Diana heard Irene answer. "I've known for some time I could walk. In fact, I have been practicing. Here, let me show you. Can you help me up?"

For the next few minutes, Diana watched as Caleb carefully helped Irene's fumbling attempts to appear a fledgling novice at walking.

Concern on his face, his voice was soothing as he spoke. "Don't try to force it. Keep your mind on just one thing, what it means to me if you can walk again. Try, please, for me!"

"It is what I've always wanted, dreamed about—us," Irene told him. "I'm sure, now that I can walk, we can have a life together."

Diana felt a razor-sharp pain somewhere in the vicinity of her heart. She closed her eyes, but the scene remained indelibly etched in her mind. Although she had been unable to see the exact expression on Caleb's face, she still could hear the joy in his voice.

Diana turned, hurrying away from the window, knowing as she went up the stairs what she had to do. *You'd better leave,* said an inner voice, *while you still can.* It was too late to avoid the pain. Caleb was like a narcotic in the blood, one she already was addicted to.

She dragged a suitcase from a closet shelf, and with an aching heart, began packing. She was hardly aware of what she was doing as she shoved things into two suitcases. Two were all she could manage, the rest could come later. Tonight she'd go, after the house was dark, when nobody would be able to see the unhappiness on her face.

After several trips down the balcony to the waiting car below she was ready to leave. Barry hardly stirred in her arms as she made the last trip to the car. She never glanced back, knowing it was a painful reminder she wished to avoid. Halfway to Vermont she called Marty and assured herself of a welcome.

Diana had expected Caleb to call—she never thought he would come after her. She might have guessed that Vermont was the first place he'd look.

She'd been sitting in the dark when she heard his car in the driveway. At least, she thought gratefully as she went to answer his knock, she was beyond tears. They had long ago dried on her cheeks and were no longer visible to the naked eye, only etched painfully inside.

"I just want to know one thing, Diana. Why?" he asked, his voice cold, his face devoid of expression as they stared at one another.

"You could have called, Caleb. There wasn't any need to come here."

Ignoring her, he repeated, "I'm waiting. Why? You saw Irene and myself talking. Couldn't you wait for an explanation?" he asked.

"Yes, I saw you. Very touching. Poor Caleb." She added, resorting to sarcasm, "So torn. By clearing out, I'm just paving the way, making it easier, so you can live there with Irene."

"Is that what you think I want?" Caleb's voice was skeptical. "You can't begin to guess what I really need! Again, I'm asking, Diana, why?"

"It just wasn't working. We both know that."

"I'm sorry to be so obtuse, but I know nothing of the kind. True, we had our problems, but most marriages do. We could have found the answers. That is if you wanted to. There's someone else, isn't there? You're still in love with Steven Brenner, aren't you? You've been seeing Steve outside of Twelve Trees. I saw you having lunch. How many times?"

"Twice." Her voice was barely above a whisper.

His next question was full of meaning. "Just for lunch? I'd rather have the truth. What does Steve Brenner mean to you?"

Diana was willing to grasp at straws, anything to make him go away before she made a fool of herself and cried. But it wasn't necessary to lie. Some of the relief must have shown on her face. It made it unnecessary to answer him.

"Never mind. I can see how much you are torn about this. I don't want you to come back unless it's what you want. Don't bother to lie! I won't ask you to return. If you come back, it will be your choice, your decision."

He turned and walked out into the night. It was two weeks later and hours of pain before she knew anything about Caleb. She called Twelve Trees. She'd left in such a rush she'd left her paints. If there was any time in her life she needed to get lost in her work, it was during this period. Painting was the only possible solution. Life looked bleak, to say the least. Barry was her only joy.

If only she could cry. She needed the release of tears, the cleansing effect she was sure they would bring. But each day passed and she remained unable to cry.

When she called about her paints, Burtie told her she'd see they were sent off. Diana noticed the cool tone in her voice. She had to know. "How is Caleb?"

"Little late asking, isn't it?" Burtie said, not giving an inch, making Diana worm every bit of information from her.

"He is my husband. I'm just curious."

"All right. I've hardly seen him. He works, he runs, he rarely eats."

"Burtie, you can make him take care of himself. Try, will you?"

After a long pause, Burtie said, "I'll try."

A couple of weeks later, Diana called again. The excuse seemed flimsy even to her ears. After a minute, she asked, "How is everyone?"

"Caleb, you mean?"

"Yes, Burtie. Caleb."

"He hasn't been feeling well."

"What's wrong?" Diana asked alarmed.

A long pause before Burtie answered, "Headaches. I'm not sure if it's tension or flu symptoms."

"Has he been to a doctor?"

"You should know Caleb better than that."

"He hasn't?"

"Correct. He won't go even if I suggested it."

"Try, will you, for me?"

"Okay." After a short pause, Burtie said, "Do you want to talk to him?"

"No. You convince him. I'll keep in touch."

"Diana," Burtie added, "I thought you might like to know. Irene's gone."

"Gone? *Gone?*" Diana repeated, a wild clamoring in her chest. Could the bane of her existence actually be out of her life?

"Yes. Sterns drove her to Scarsdale yesterday. Her sister lives there."

"What did Caleb do about it?"

"Nothing. What did you expect him to do?"

"Will she be back?"

"From the heated words I overheard, I doubt it very much. He made her an allowance, a very small one by her standards." Burtie chuckled. "It wasn't exactly what she'd expected." She asked again, "Are you sure you don't want to speak to him?"

"No. Let me know how he is?"

Each time she called, Burtie told her of Caleb's progressively worsening condition until Diana couldn't handle it any longer. She would leave early in the morning.

Any other time she would have enjoyed visiting with Marty, Jeff, and the boys. But under the circumstances, she only wanted to be one place. Welcome or not, she was going home to Twelve Trees.

Diana let herself silently into the house, somehow feeling almost like an intruder. Quietly she walked toward the kitchen, fairly sure this was where she'd find someone. She wasn't disappointed.

Lottie was loading the breakfast dishes in the dishwasher while Mrs. Warburton was peeling vegetables at the sink. At one end of the kitchen table Sterns was at his never-ending polishing of the silver. It was he who saw Diana first.

"Why, Mrs. B., what a surprise!" Sterns exclaimed, his usual unexpressive face breaking into a wide smile. "A very welcome surprise, I might add."

Lottie and Burtie both turned simultaneously on hearing his words. Lottie gave a squeal of delight while Burtie reproached her with a look, saying, her voice full of censure, "It's about time, I'd say."

Diana sat Barry down. He, too, had let out a chortle of laughter on seeing Lottie. He toddled to her, mouthing "Ottie" as he went.

"Where is Caleb?" Diana asked.

"He's running around the lake," Sterns replied.

"It's raining! Are you sure that's where he is? He's ill!"

As Diana watched the blank expressions on Sterns's and Lottie's faces, she realized Burtie had tricked her about Caleb's being ill. She also saw the self-satisfied smugness apparent in Burtie's face.

"The rain wouldn't stop him," Sterns answered. "He's always running."

Burtie had been studying Diana during this exchange. She could feel the probing look, knowing Burtie was speculating as to why she was here. "He's trying to run away from something," Burtie stated sternly, the disapproval still there in her voice. "Unhappiness I'd say, if I'm any judge."

Although she didn't say so, she clearly felt Diana was the main cause of it. "He won't eat hardly anything. I can't tempt him with any of his favorite treats."

"Treat? Cookie?" Barry piped, looking at Burtie who usually kept the cookie jar full. As Lottie handed him a cookie, Diana asked, "Would you watch Barry for me?"

"Do you intend to stay?" Burtie wanted to know. "If you don't, Caleb would be better off if you just turn around and walk out of here!"

180

This statement brought an underlying gasp from both Sterns and Lottie. They were amazed at her audacity though Diana wasn't. Burtie continued, adding, "Caleb keeps it inside, never lets anyone see how he hurts. But he can't keep it from me. I've known him too long. Are you going to stay?"

"I want to." Diana's eyes stung, tears close to the surface. "If he'll let me!"

"He'll let you," Burtie stated gruffly, "or answer to me. Now go find him and don't bring him back till all is healed between you."

Diana smiled her thanks before leaving by the back door.

The rain was heavier now. But it didn't even cause her a moment's hesitation as she took off in the direction of the lake. Her eyes scanned the edge, spying Caleb, a distant figure on the opposite shore.

Soon into the run, her breath labored with the exertion. It seemed to take forever to shorten the distance between them. *Please,* she thought, her mind racing ahead, *let him ask me to stay.* The idea that Caleb might reject her sent a shiver of fear coursing up her spine.

Ahead she saw him, closer now. She realized painfully that life would be over without him. She'd been the one who had walked out six weeks ago. He had so little tolerance for human frailties. Setting high standards for himself, he expected the same of others. Somehow, she had to convince him of what he meant to her, make him forgive her and want her again.

Diana waved her arm and shouted. He was still far enough away so she couldn't see his exact features, but he stopped. Diana stopped, too, glued to the spot. She could almost sense his amazement, his eyes disbelieving what he saw.

Later, neither one was sure who made the first move,

but suddenly they were both running toward each other. While Caleb seemed to be flying at lightning-swift speed, Diana felt as if she were traveling in slow motion—a snail's pace compared to what she wanted to do.

Once she was in his arms, he whirled her around and around, showering her face with kisses till both of them were dizzy with the exertion. Held tightly against him, Diana breathed deeply, panting from both the run and the exhilaration of being with Caleb again. Within the circle of his arms, Diana's eyes locked with Caleb's, hers the clearest emerald green, bright with unshed tears, his the deepest brown, watchful as he looked at his wife.

"Tears?" he scoffed softly. "Not my Diana. It must be the rain."

"It's not the rain," she whispered, her voice husky. Afraid, but knowing she must have an answer, Diana added, "Caleb, can I come back?"

Her eyes never left his. There was a plea in her voice.

Wiping away the tears with his finger and pushing back the damp ringlets of her hair, he studied her face. The corner of his mouth turned up, smiling at her disheveled appearance.

"You don't actually think I'd let you go again, do you?"

Then his mouth was on hers, blotting out everything and every thought with it.

It was the insistent fall of the rain, harder now, that finally made them break apart. The nearest shelter was the summerhouse and neither needed prompting from the other to head in its direction.

With a sense of déjà vu, she watched Caleb pull the cushions from the benches, raising the lid once more to collect the beach towels stored inside. He tossed one to

Diana, spreading the other two on the cushions before using one on his own damp head. She watched as he pulled his T-shirt over his head, mopping the curly hair on his chest before throwing it carelessly in a corner.

"You're soaked through, Diana. Get out of those wet things," he said, nodding meaningfully at her clothes. Then he said, his gaze shifting to her face as he watched her, "You aren't shy, are you?"

"Of course not," she retorted. Nonetheless, she turned her back to him before taking off her shirt, pants and tennis shoes. She wrapped the folds of the huge towel around herself, conscious of the skimpy wisps of her bra and panties. It was hard to meet his eyes when she turned around. Lifting a questioning brow, he made no comment, but merely offered her a place beside him on the cushions.

"I have something to tell you. A discovery I've made recently." Caleb pulled a letter from the pocket of his jogging shorts. "Here, I've been carrying this around wondering how I was going to get you to read it. I wanted you back because of other reasons—not this. Hard as it is to admit, it's given me an insight into myself I'd just as soon hadn't been revealed. I saw myself through my brother's eyes and it wasn't very complimentary. Burtie found it tucked away in a book among some of Barrett's things."

Diana unfolded the piece of paper, but before she started to read it, Caleb stopped her, adding, "Before you begin I want you to know one thing. Irene is gone. And she won't be back to interfere in our lives ever again. You were right about several things. The main one—she can walk, and very well."

"Before I read this I have a confession to make." Her face warmed under the questioning gaze. "Remember how I tried to make you believe there was something between Steve and me? Well . . ." She hesitated, the color deepening, "we were never more than good friends."

"I know. Last week I met Steve with Suzanne, and she had a diamond on the appropriate finger."

Diana felt enough guilt to look a bit chagrined before her eyes dropped to the letter in her hand and she began to read.

Deanna, my love,

Just a few hastily scribbled lines. I wanted you to have this bank passbook in your possession. Most of the things in my New Haven apartment will go into storage till we have a home of our own. I was afraid this might get mixed up in the move, especially with such weighty matters on my mind.

I've spoken with Irene again and it still looks bleak. Why I ever let my brother railroad me into this mess, I'll never know. A "Buchanan" heir would never have come from this union. Irene did, however, agree to drive to Woodledge on Saturday and discuss a possible settlement. Maybe, if it's large enough, she'll consent to a divorce. As a last resort I could show her your letters about the baby. They're still in their hiding place in the desk.

Caleb called last night from London. He naturally talked to Irene first thing. No telling what she told him.

He's coming home on the first available plane.

He's going to know a few home truths about Irene and our so-called marriage. I wish he'd married that block of ice, instead of me.

Perhaps I shouldn't be so hard on him. He

was older, more affected by Mother's desertion and Dad's drinking than I was. Still I wish he'd run his life and leave mine alone.

By the way, I went to see Mother yesterday. She and her husband live in a New Haven suburb. She wants to meet you. Caleb should make the effort to see her once in a while, too. She wants a reconciliation, but Caleb has a very unforgiving nature.

We will make a special place for her in our lives. I'm sorry I missed you, my love. I'll call again tomorrow. Take care of yourself and our babe.

I'll love you always,

Barry

Everything Barrett had ever revealed to Diana about his marriage was contained in that missive. She raised her gaze from the piece of paper, unsure what mood Caleb would be in.

"In giving you that," Caleb said with a rueful smile, "I laid myself wide open for an 'I told you so.' Everything you've been trying to tell me about my brother's marriage is in there."

Diana stated, "You aren't the only one who did the wrong thing. That reference to a missed call—I told him she wasn't there! Only she was. I thought it best to try and play God. It was the last time she would have spoken to him. He died the next day. The guilt I've had to live with. . . ."

"The past is past, Diana. Feeling guilty won't change it."

"I know, only I wish I hadn't kept the call from her just the same." With the emotion in her voice, she had trouble speaking above a whisper.

"I wonder why this wasn't mailed?" Diana mused.

"I can't be sure, of course," Caleb speculated. "He was moving. It was shoved between the pages of a book and forgotten."

Suddenly Diana remembered something about the night Barrett died. "Was it *Sonnets from the Portuguese?*" she asked, curious.

"Why, yes, I think it was! How . . . ?"

"The night Barrett died he told the ambulance attendant to tell Deanna to read them." Diana's voice was so full of tears she could only whisper, "Dee read them over and over thinking there was some hidden meaning. She decided he must have meant their love was like Elizabeth Barrett's and Robert Browning's."

" 'How do I love thee? Let me count the ways,' " he quoted softly, tugging on her hair, allowing a damp ringlet to curl around his finger. When she wouldn't meet his eyes, he lifted her chin, and said, his voice full, "It fits, you know. I couldn't have said it better."

Her eyes a luminous green, she stared. Had he just said . . . ?

He cupped his hand around the back of her neck, letting his other hand trail intimately along her shoulder, stopping at the towel. "It doesn't matter if you don't love me yet. I love you enough for both of us."

"Not love you, sweet fool. What do you suppose this crazy ache is then?" She looked at him then, letting all the love, the tender feeling shine through, wanting him to see.

She reached out a hand; the raspy feel of his unshaved face sent shivers along her spine. Warmth crept into her face as she caught the amused look on his. He'd read her thoughts, quite accurately.

"Burtie told me you were ill. I came running home, expecting to find you on the way to the hospital."

"I have a champion there." His grin was young and boyish. "You'd better be good to me. She'll see you

186

do." Then his eyes changed to a dark intense look, a look that did funny things to her insides. "Where do we go from here?" he smiled, loving her with his eyes.

"I guess back to pick up the pieces of our life together. Build on it, make it better. Barry has been asking about you."

Diana shivered but not from the cool air. It was true the breeze was chilly, damp air filling the summerhouse, the rain keeping up its steady rant on the roof. His dark eyes watched her, smiling at her shyness.

"Barry can wait."

"Caleb! Someone might see. It's broad daylight!" Diana was alarmed as he tugged at the towel. But feeble attempts were futile against his superior strength and steadfast purpose of mind.

"If they do, and I doubt it, they'll leave quickly enough. Diana, stop fighting me. It has been six long weeks!"

His mouth blotted out any more protests that might have been forthcoming. Somehow, later, it all seemed so right—the final healing coming during a storm. Even as it raged outside, their loving had been full of promise.

Silhouette Romance

IT'S YOUR OWN SPECIAL TIME

Contemporary romances for today's women.
Each month, six very special love stories will be yours
from SILHOUETTE. Look for them wherever books are sold
or order now from the coupon below.

$1.50 each

Hampson	☐ 1	☐ 4	☐ 16	☐ 27		Browning	☐ 12	☐ 38	☐ 53	☐ 73
	☐ 28	☐ 52	☐ 94				☐ 93			
Stanford	☐ 6	☐ 25	☐ 35	☐ 46		Michaels	☐ 15	☐ 32	☐ 61	☐ 87
	☐ 58	☐ 88				John	☐ 17	☐ 34	☐ 57	☐ 85
Hastings	☐ 13	☐ 26				Beckman	☐ 8	☐ 37	☐ 54	☐ 96
Vitek	☐ 33	☐ 47	☐ 84			Wisdom	☐ 49	☐ 95		
Wildman	☐ 29	☐ 48				Halston	☐ 62	☐ 83		

☐ 5 Goforth	☐ 22 Stephens	☐ 50 Scott	☐ 81 Roberts
☐ 7 Lewis	☐ 23 Edwards	☐ 55 Ladame	☐ 82 Dailey
☐ 9 Wilson	☐ 24 Healy	☐ 56 Trent	☐ 86 Adams
☐ 10 Caine	☐ 30 Dixon	☐ 59 Vernon	☐ 89 James
☐ 11 Vernon	☐ 31 Halldorson	☐ 60 Hill	☐ 90 Major
☐ 14 Oliver	☐ 36 McKay	☐ 63 Brent	☐ 92 McKay
☐ 19 Thornton	☐ 39 Sinclair	☐ 71 Ripy	☐ 97 Clay
☐ 20 Fulford	☐ 43 Robb	☐ 76 Hardy	☐ 98 St. George
☐ 21 Richards	☐ 45 Carroll	☐ 78 Oliver	☐ 99 Camp

$1.75 each

Stanford	☐ 100	☐ 112	☐ 131		Browning	☐ 113	☐ 142	☐ 164	
Hardy	☐ 101	☐ 130			Michaels	☐ 114	☐ 146		
Cork	☐ 103	☐ 148			Beckman	☐ 124	☐ 154		
Vitek	☐ 104	☐ 139	☐ 157		Roberts	☐ 127	☐ 143	☐ 163	
Dailey	☐ 106	☐ 118	☐ 153		Trent	☐ 110	☐ 161		
Bright	☐ 107	☐ 125			Wisdom	☐ 132	☐ 166		
Hampson	☐ 108	☐ 119	☐ 128	☐ 136	Hunter	☐ 137	☐ 167		
	☐ 147	☐ 151	☐ 155	☐ 160	Scott	☐ 117	☐ 169		

Silhouette Desire
15-Day Trial Offer
A new romance series
that explores
contemporary relationships
in exciting detail

Six Silhouette Desire romances, free for 15 days!
We'll send you six new Silhouette Desire romances
to look over for 15 days, absolutely free! If you decide
not to keep the books, return them and owe nothing.

Six books a month, free home delivery. If you like
Silhouette Desire romances as much as we think you
will, keep them and return your payment with the
invoice. Then we will send you six new books every
month to preview, just as soon as they are published.
You pay only for the books you decide to keep, and
you never pay postage and handling.

Silhouette Romance

Coming next month from
Silhouette Romances

Dark Fantasy by Laura Hardy

Lisa Hayley, a successful actress, thought she had everything.
Then she met James Tarrant and became involved in a real-life
drama where she longed to make her own happy ending.

To Buy A Memory by Anne Hampson

How could Loretta have fallen for a perfect stranger who
deliberately toyed with her emotions? Yet Paul's kisses were
commanding and soon she found herself past caring.

Love Is Elected by Alyssa Howard

Kara realized she wasn't immune to Matthew Jordan's
charms, but could she really be hopelessly in love with the man
who took her for a wife . . . in name only?

Moonlit Magic by Joanna Scott

Interior designer Timi Johnston had fallen in love with a
Mexican nobleman and found herself in a world where an
independent young career woman definitely didn't fit in.

Sweet Jasmine by Jeanne Stephens

Brook Adamson befriended a lonely little girl—millionaire Dane
Darcy's daughter. But soon that friendship led to a passionate
love for Dane who remained cynical of her motives.

No More Regrets by Dorothy Cork

Once rejected by the only man she had ever loved,
Alida now found herself in his employ—with the attraction
as strong as ever and her heart too willing!